A Candlelight Ecstasy Romance®

LEANING BACK IN THE CRADLE OF HIS ARMS, SHE WATCHED FOR A TRIUMPHANT SMILE. . . .

There was none. The fullness of his lips were rewarded by the cool softness of her own mouth. The hands at her back trembled but continued on their enticing path.

"Kiss me," she said. She'd never asked before. Jaycee wasn't prepared for the explosion that followed. His lips fused and sealed over hers. Behind closed lids, the Fourth of July fireworks had begun ahead of schedule. She'd read about rockets exploding but had thought it poppycock. It wasn't. Multicolored bursts ignited a passion that brought a primeval groan from her soul.

A CANDLELIGHT ECSTASY ROMANCE®

KISS THE TEARS AWAY

Anna Hudson

A CANDLELIGHT ECSTASY ROMANCE®

Published by
Dell Publishing Co., Inc.
1 Dag Hammarskjold Plaza
New York, New York 10017

Dell ® TM 681510, Dell Publishing Co., Inc.

Candlelight Ecstasy Romance®, 1,203,540, is a registered
trademark of Dell Publishing Co., Inc.,
New York, New York.

ISBN: 0-440-14525-2

Printed in the United States of America
First printing—July 1983

Dedicated with love to

My father, who taught me to dream,
My husband, who made the dream possible,
My children, who are learning to dream themselves.

To Our Readers:

We have been delighted with your enthusiastic response to Candlelight Ecstasy Romances®, and we thank you for the interest you have shown in this exciting series.

In the upcoming months we will continue to present the distinctive, sensuous love stories you have come to expect only from Ecstasy. We look forward to bringing you many more books from your favorite authors and also the very finest work from new authors of contemporary romantic fiction.

As always, we are striving to present the unique absorbing love stories that you enjoy most—books that are more than ordinary romance.

Your suggestions and comments are always welcome. Please write to us at the address below.

Sincerely,

The Editors
Candlelight Romances
1 Dag Hammarskjold Plaza
New York, New York 10017

CHAPTER ONE

"Little girl, is your daddy around?" a well-modulated tenor voice asked.

The tip of her pencil snapped under the pressure of Jaycee Warner's fingers as she sat hunched over her desk. Since that rotten "Short People" song had been aired on radio and television, she'd been the brunt of a thousand and one bad jokes.

Raising a well-scrubbed face, but keeping her shoulders hunched, she answered pitifully, "Daddy left Mom for another woman." *Think of another cutesy remark,* she thought, directing a glare at the belt at eye level, then raising her eyes higher to watch a blush creep from under a stiffly starched white collar.

Jaycee's deep chocolate eyes rounded; the hidden copper flecks flared as she followed the red path. The man confronting her was beautiful! Not feminine; but godlike. Golden hair, streaked white from the sun, the deepest of silver-gray eyes, a finely chiseled nose and mouth, and a body any construction worker would envy stood uncomfortably before her. But best of all, he was well under six feet tall.

A broad grin split Jaycee's face. This was as unexpected as a free load of copper delivered to the shop. All consternation over the tedious bookkeeping she'd been forced to do fled. She stared appreciatively, memorizing each physical detail.

The stranger recovered his composure, dropped his briefcase to the floor, and leaned over the desk. Sympathy clouded his face. "I'm sorry, young lady." Straightening, he asked gently, "Is the owner around?"

A melodious laugh tinkled through Jaycee's lips. Mentally she debated whether or not to continue the charade. Why not? They could laugh about it later over a drink.

Shaking her head, which swung the long honey-colored ponytail over her shoulder, she answered in a childish falsetto voice. "Not so's you'd notice."

Displeasure flashed over the handsome features. Reaching into his billfold, the intruder extracted a business card and placed it on the green blotter covering the desktop.

"It's important that I see him right away." A definite gruff quality distorted the smooth tenor that was first in the voice.

Jaycee read the card silently. JONATHAN WYNTHROP, INTERNAL REVENUE SERVICE, ST. LOUIS, MISSOURI. *Cr-i-i-ips! The IRS! What did they want? Nothing good,* she quickly answered herself. They wouldn't be laughing about anything over a drink.

Precariously Jaycee Warner leaned back in her old-fashioned chair. She watched the concerned expression change to one of disbelief as the buttons on her navy blue jumpsuit strained to contain her ample breasts.

"You're a woman," the man stated in apparent disbelief.

"Astute observation, Mr. Wynthrop," Jaycee quipped dryly. Her sharp tongue firmly in place, she asked, "What can I do for you?"

"Do you work for Jaycee Plumbing Company?"

"I *am* Jaycee Plumbing Company."

"You mean you run the office," he said, trying to clarify her specific duties.

"Wrong again. I run copper water pipe, usually in apartment projects. Sometimes plastic, but not often. PVC glue stinks." Invasion by the IRS didn't warrant subtlety. Her emphasis on the word *stinks* clearly indicated her attitude.

Jonathan Wynthrop's silver eyes frosted over as they reassessed Jaycee's heart-shaped face. One sweep skimmed over the large dark eyes, the up-turned nose sprinkled lightly with freckles, and the wide, generous mouth. Her hostility was blatantly evident.

"You've ignored our warning letters, Ms. Warner."

"I didn't receive them," she retorted.

They never do, telepathed across the desk unspoken. The lifting of the corner of one lip spoke volumes. The raised eyebrow radioed the message loud and clear.

Bending from the waist, Jonathan retrieved his dark leather briefcase. Simultaneously the latches clicked open. He handed two official documents to Jaycee.

"The government is seizing the company bank account and"—a large padlock and hasp clunked on the desk—"locks will be placed on your doors." Distaste edged each clipped phrase.

The chair squeaked loudly, protesting the rapid movement as Jaycee returned it to its customary position. "Damn it. There's been a mistake!" She waved one hand, rejecting the condemning papers as her renowned temper soared out of control.

Disregarding the interruption and the dismissive gesture, Jonathan slipped the sheets of paper beneath his calling card. Completing the task, he picked up the padlock and hasp and headed toward the front door.

"All contents will be auctioned off, as stated in the court order. The proceeds, hopefully, will cover your debt." His voice droned on as a taped recording of a telephone message does.

Jaycee sprung around the desk. Grasping his elbow, she forcibly swung him around. "Now, just a damned minute you . . ." she sputtered, seeking the appropriate derogatory term, ". . . you TAX COLLECTOR!" The way she said it made the name sound like the foulest expletive ever heard.

Glacial ice covered the silver eyes, making them the color of solder. Their piercing quality riveted on the small fingers wadding his jacket sleeve but the pint-sized spitfire defied his withering look.

He may close my shop down, she thought, fuming,

14

but he's going to hear what I think of people in his profession. I'll have that satisfaction at least.

Jerking his arm, she spat out, "You know, our forefathers, the founders of this country, knew what to do with your kind of riffraff. Agents were tarred and feathered; their wives were raped; then the whole kit and kaboodle was run out of town on a rail."

Diverting her attention by dropping the lock, with a quick upward motion Jonathan freed his sleeve from her grasp. Using the unrestrained hand, he removed a small pad and pencil from the breast pocket of his dark pinstriped suit.

"Now. Let's make certain I understand your statement. I'm to be tarred and feathered." The pencil flashed over the white pad. "You're going to rape my wife. . . . Since I'm not married that should prove difficult, not to mention your"—amused eyes raked her figure—"lack of equipment. And for a finale you're going to run me out of town on a rail."

The look she received indicated she would be the one leaving town. Sent up the river to the nearest federal prison.

"You didn't intend to use rape as a bribe, did you?" Audaciously he smiled. "My partner is in the display room. You'd have to include him in on any offer."

On the inside Jaycee's temper reached an all-time high, but the mask she wore was one of icy disdain.

"I thought not," he said with mock disappointment.

Realizing she was losing in the battle of words, she

changed tactics. Pivoting away toward the door, Jaycee laughed loudly and coarsely.

"Get your partner in here. Snakes always travel in pairs, don't they?" she insulted.

Jonathan Wynthrop stood silently.

Pushing past him, Jaycee stepped into the display room. The other tax agent was twisting the handle on a Moen sink fixture. His index finger pushed his wire-framed glasses into place as he stooped over and peered up into the faucet.

"You aren't expecting water to come out, are you?" Jaycee asked caustically. Normally she treated a prospective client with the utmost courtesy, but this odious creature was just another tax agent. Jaycee stifled a giggle when the agent's head clunked into the chrome spigot. *Klutz.*

"No . . . ah, I was looking for the thingumabob you use to attach between the faucet and a portable dishwasher." Straightening to his full height, he towered over Jaycee's small figure. *No problem,* she thought. *He, too, can be whittled down to size.*

"The thingumabob is called an adapter and they're in the boxes behind the counter," Jaycee replied, gesturing toward the myriad small boxes orderly stacked behind the glass case. "Can I sell you one before you padlock the door? Or would you rather buy it for fifty cents on the dollar at the government auction?" she asked with false sweetness.

The tall agent had the grace to flush.

"Hostile owner," she heard from the office door.

"Another astute observation, Mr. Wynthrop. You have a knack for stating the obvious," she snapped.

Hands on hips, she turned and glared. "I told you that this is all a mistake, but you arrogant bastards . . ."

"I believe in the plumbing trade that is called a toilet tongue," Jonathan interjected before Jaycee could string together more abusive language.

"Stop, Jonathan!" The command was issued authoritatively from his older partner. "Let me explain the facts, young lady. After repeated warnings, you have not complied with the laws governing the paying of withholding taxes. According to our records, you are three years delinquent. Is that correct?"

"Absolutely not! If you will just . . ."

"The IRS doesn't make mistakes," Jonathan interjected in a bored tone.

"Well, this time you have." Jaycee dropped the pitch of her voice. This technique was more effective than ranting, wailing, and gnashing her teeth. She controlled the urge to do all three. "Kindly refrain from interrupting me, Mr. Wynthrop. Only your rudeness surpasses your stupidity." Righteous indignation made the sentence trail off to a whisper. Pointing to Jonathan's partner, she continued. "Let me call my accountant. He'll straighten this mess out."

Jaycee watched as the agents sent silent signals to each other. Shrugging his shoulders and glancing at his watch, Jonathan indicated it would be a waste of time. With dark, eloquent eyes Jaycee pleaded with the older agent to take the time. Jonathan's partner nodded his head. He'd make the call.

Delving into his jacket pocket, he pulled out a packet of business cards. "I'm Larry Dettrick."

"Jaycee Warner. Thanks," she responded, accepting the card. Nervously she flicked the corner of the object she'd just received.

The three of them returned to the office. Jaycee moved behind the desk and flipped open her black telephone directory. Dialing the number of her accountant, Jaycee looked up at the conservatively dressed men. The phone buzzed in her ear. Once. Twice. Jaycee tapped her fingers impatiently. *Be there, Scotty,* she prayed.

"Scott Lang here."

"Jaycee Warner. I have a problem." Meticulously, step by step, she related what had happened. She eliminated the verbal warfare that had taken place and the threats she'd made. Distress marred the melodious quality of her voice.

"It's an error of some sort. Probably a computer misprint. Let me speak to one of the agents," Scott said calmly, trying to soothe his agitated client. "Calm down, Jaycee, and for heaven's sake don't lose your temper."

Too late for that advice, she thought, handing the phone to Larry Dettrick and gesturing for him to be seated at the desk.

"Thank you," Larry murmured politely before sinking into the squeaky chair and placing the receiver to his ear.

Striding out of the office, Jaycee began pacing the crowded display area. Wringing small, callused hands, she considered the possibilities. Louise, her office manager, faithfully filled out the numerous forms the government required. Well, maybe she'd fudge a little here and there, but what businessman didn't? Could Louise have made a series of mistakes? She shook her head, her ponytail swishing over her shoulders.

Louise had been Jaycee's dad's secretary for twenty years. She was competent. A right-hand man. She was practically family. Surrogate mother, confidante, and friend were only a few personal attributes labeling Louise. Over the years she had bandaged Jaycee's scuffed knees, wiped tears, and given sage advice. The chubby middle-aged woman had been the person who had encouraged her to become a plumber when her own mother had covered her face and wept at the decision.

Scotty had to be right. The computer must have screwed up. Wasn't she frequently hearing about computers making disastrous printouts? The back of Jaycee's neck tingled.

Without looking, she knew Jonathan Wynthrop was close. She turned, anticipating a decision that would be the lethal blow to her business. She inhaled deeply, held her breath, and waited.

"Will you accept my apology for baiting you earlier?" he asked. He had removed his jacket and stood with one hand thrust into his pants pocket. She could hear the change in his pocket jingle.

"You mean the mighty IRS agent, representative of white-haired Uncle Sam, made a mistake?" she queried scathingly.

"No, but I should have handled you"—his eyes swept from her head to her feet—"more professionally. Hostile owners don't usually get under my skin."

"Postmen *handle* mail. Trainers *handle* dogs. You will *never* handle me." Eyes narrowing, they shot out copper sparks. "*I* handle plumbing problems. I'm an independent contractor . . ."

"And an independent lady," Jonathan added.

"Right. For the first time since you've been here. Independent *and* a lady. Men don't handle ladies. Even your apology was damned insulting."

"Ladies don't curse. Maybe I should have just said independent." Exasperation threaded through his voice.

"If you accomplish your goal, I won't be independent either. You'll put me right out of business. Do you know what will happen if you put a lock on my door? Within an hour the phone will ring off the wall. Suppliers will be calling wanting to know if they'll be paid. Contractors will harass me for liens. Bid proposals from Jaycee Plumbing will be thrown in the wastebasket. I might as well take my master's license and rip it in half." She panted slightly from the long-winded speech and waved her hand toward the official documents hanging behind the counter.

Her voice lowered. "Mister, I've worked for six long years for my independence. I've stood in icy water up to my knees repairing burst watermains during a winter ice storm. On a summer day like today, putting the striker to the torch increases the heat around you ten degrees. And you have the nerve to stand in this air-conditioned office, dressed impeccably, and make jibes about my being a lady?"

Jaycee could feel tears of rage gathering behind her eyelids. She wouldn't cry. She never cried. Thrusting her rounded chin forward, she laughed hoarsely.

"Take your apology and shove it. How's that for unladylike?" The unshed tears streaming down the back of her throat formed an unpassable lump.

"Jaycee . . ." The agent began closing the gap between them.

"Stay away from me, you puffed-up, pompous ass. There aren't enough dirty words in a sewer for a tax collector like you," she said. Shakily her hands covered her face.

"What's going on?" she heard Agent Dettrick ask.

Swallowing, Jaycee cleared her throat of the blockage. "A hostile owner becoming hysterical," she answered, realizing she'd taken her fears out on the other agent. "Was it a mistake?" she asked hopefully.

"You're in the clear . . . temporarily. Mr. Lang has put enough doubt into my mind that I can't justifiably shut down your shop or freeze your bank account. You can thank the Fourth of July weekend for the reprieve. I won't be able to check out Lang's theory until next week, when the computers are available." Larry sighed, as though speaking for any length of time was a tremendous effort.

Jaycee could have wept for joy. It might only be temporary, but it was a reprieve. Between Louise and Scotty they could find the receipts that would prove payment. No one need know that the government had paid her a visit.

"Thank you, Mr. Dettrick. You don't know the amount of anguish you've saved me by agreeing to make that phone call." The sincerity of her appreciation glowed from the copper flecks in her dark brown eyes.

"I'm sorry if we've inconvenienced you." A wide smile spread over his face. "Is there a chance you'd sell me one of those whatchamacallits? My wife has nagged at me for weeks to get it taken care of."

She'd have given him the adapter, but the fear that his partner would construe it as a bribe halted her natural generosity.

"My pleasure, Mr. Dettrick."

Nimble fingers slid the box holding a dozen adapters off the shelf. She selected one and placed it in the palm of the agent's hand.

"Including tax that's seven fifty-nine."

"Will you take a personal check?"

"Certainly. If you can't trust an IRS agent, who can you trust?" she asked cheekily.

The transaction completed, Jaycee pulled out the cash register drawer, put the check away, and stuck a business card forward.

"Call me when you need a good, competent plumber."

"Thanks. I'll do that." Accepting the card, he tucked it into his breast pocket.

"Larry, would you mind waiting in the car for a moment? I'd like to speak to Ms. Warner alone for a minute."

Jonathan had silently moved beside his partner. Apprehensively Larry glanced from Jonathan to

Jaycee, raising an eyebrow. Jaycee nodded her head in agreement.

"Well, thanks for the whatsit," he said warmly. "I'll be talking to you next week."

Jonathan stood on the other side of the counter. When Jaycee raised her head, she caught the full force of bright silver eyes trying to penetrate beneath the business pose she'd assumed. Blood circulated through her veins as though she'd attached a five horsepower pump to her heart.

"Would you accept my apology over dinner tonight?" One hand slid forward and covered hers.

The cool glass beneath and the warmth emanating from his touch caused a fogprint to appear on the sleek glass surface. The pump malfunctioned; her heart skipped a beat. This man was dangerous, not only to her business, but to her personal well-being. If he was heartless enough to put a padlock on her door, he'd have no qualms about destroying her.

"I'll accept your apology now and save you the price of a meal."

Her hand flattened against the cool glass before she felt him gently lift and stroke her inner wrist with his thumb. Could he tell how irregular her heartbeat was by touching this pulse point?

"I still would enjoy taking you to dinner, Jaycee. Say yes," he coaxed persuasively.

She abruptly laughed in his face. The old defense mechanism was properly functioning. Seeking to wound, she said, "Mister, a poorly paid government employee can't afford me."

The physical violence of slapping his face would

23

have had less impact. Jonathan jolted away, his eyes burning angrily as though ignited by her refusal.

Recovering from the verbal onslaught, Jonathan smiled sardonically. Sloughing off the words as beneath contempt, he answered softly. "I'll save up and come back."

Briefcase in hand, he slowly sauntered to the door as if nothing unpleasant had happened. With a mock salute he left.

Holding herself erect, Jaycee walked back into the office and sat behind the desk. She had won both the battle and the war, hadn't she? It wasn't in character for her to allow a man past those defensive barriers she'd firmly built over the years. Jonathan had attacked the inner walls, but they weren't breached. Why did she have the urge to bury her head in her arms and bawl like a baby? She hadn't felt this miserable in ages.

Her defense mechanisms of laughter and a sharp tongue were the direct result of the shame and humiliation she had experienced during her teenage years when her female hormones had revolted against her tomboy ways. All together they had screamed, "Stop secreting" for height and "*Go-go-go*" for bust development. The end result? A very short, extremely busty, miserable teenager.

Few boys in high school remembered climbing trees and skipping rocks across the pond with Jaycee. They didn't see that the scruffy face had become angelic. What they did see, they grabbed, groped, and speculated about. "Boom-Boom" became a much hated nickname that stuck. After a few dates that ended in wrestling matches, she decided boys simply weren't worth the hassle.

Girls were viciously cruel. Gym class was a daily horror. Jaycee tightened her bra straps until there were permanent grooves on her collar bone in an effort to keep from jiggling up and down. The effort was wasted. They bounced.

In high school she became the classic example of an underachiever, scoring well on unpublicized standardized tests, but performing poorly in class. Raising a hand to answer questions drew attention. Test grades were posted for everyone to see. That was the last thing she wanted.

Only Ruth Kline and Ruth's younger brother, Tom, the kids living next door, offered steady, unfailing friendship. But regardless of their placating remarks, she often wept in the seclusion of her bedroom.

But being different must build character, she reflected. After scraping through high school, she entered the union plumber's apprentice program. That put steel in her backbone. Three generations of family members being in the building trades gave Jaycee a natural aptitude for anything mechanical. But her stature and femininity weren't appreciated in the male-dominated apprentice program.

The icy reserve, the standoffish distrust of men, were reinforced by a few sexual encounters bordering on rape. Male coworkers speculated openly about her bountiful figure but backed off upon receiving the rough side of her tongue. She met their frustrated looks with a smirk. Sexual frustration was their prob-

lem, not hers. Jaycee decided she couldn't find love
. . . only lust.

The shrill ringing of the telephone broke through
the painful memories. Just as well, Jaycee thought.
Damn Jonathan Wynthrop for stirring up the past.

"Jaycee Plumbing. May I help you?"

"Hi, lady. All set for the weekend?"

*Dear Ruth. We're so close she probably knew I
needed her,* Jaycee thought upon recognizing the
voice.

"Sure thing. Three fun-filled days in God's country," Jaycee responded warmly.

"Do you mind if Scotty comes down Saturday
night for the fireworks?" Ruth asked.

"No. I'll give him a buzz. When are you going to
lasso my friendly CPA and put him out of his misery?" Jaycee teased. Scotty and Ruth had dated off
and on for years.

"Whenever he asks." Ruth sighed, then groaned.
"Getting him to the altar will be *the* major achieve-
ment of my life. On my tombstone they'll write,
'Here lies Ruth Klein . . . she died trying. Cause of
death . . . unrequited love.' "

"Come on, Ruth. You know he loves you," Jaycee
reassured her friend.

"I know it, and you know it, but Scotty doesn't
know it. That's the problem."

They both chuckled.

"Jaycee, I've got to run. I'm supposed to be on
potty patrol right now. Be sure you call Scotty. Tom
and I won't get to the lake until after midnight, so
don't wait up. Bye."

A school bell rang in the background as Ruth hung up the phone. Talking to Ruth never failed to bring a smile to her lips. Crazy, loveable Ruth! Her greatest fear in life was becoming an old maid schoolteacher.

"Not likely," Jaycee muttered while dialing Scotty's number. "Men!" Rolling her eyes to the ceiling in exasperation, she waited for the ring to be answered.

"Scott Lang."

"Jaycee again. I called for two reasons. First to thank you for getting the IRS off my back, and secondly to invite you to the lake tomorrow night for the fireworks display."

"Hon, I don't know what happened regarding the IRS problem, and yes, I'd love to join you at the lake. Actually I've already bought my sparklers. The gang always meets at the lake for the Fourth and I assumed you'd just forgotten to ask me. Ruth and Tom are going, aren't they?"

"Of course." Jaycee answered matter-of-factly.

"We'll discuss our strategy with the IRS Sunday morning over a fishing pole. Listen, Jaycee, I've another client walking in the door. See you Saturday around sixish. Okay?"

"Fine, but I'd rather you didn't say anything to Ruth and Tom about the business problems. See you Saturday, old fishing buddy."

"Bye," Scotty responded chuckling.

"Bye."

They'd passed a ten-dollar bill back and forth for years. Whoever caught the most fish kept the monetary prize. Presently Jaycee held the green trophy. With luck, she'd keep it for another year.

After locking the front door and placing the CLOSED sign in the window, Jaycee headed out the back toward the garage. The sight of JAYCEE PLUMB-ING emblazoned in red letters over the length of the white van never failed to lift her spirits. This was the newest addition to the company's fleet of five. Business was good. She'd doubled the profits in the three years since her father had retired and moved to Phoenix. If she stayed on course, she'd be sole owner in another three years. She twisted the key in the ignition. Imagination flashed an image of Jonathan Wynthrop on the windshield.

"You'll never close this shop," she vowed vehemently. Gunning the motor, she erased the image.

CHAPTER TWO

Tiptoeing, trying to avoid waking Ruth and Tom, Jaycee left the villa and headed toward the private boat dock. She wanted to beat the fisherman's curse, water skiers, to the best fishing spot on the lake.

Misty swirls of fog hovered over the warm lake waters. After pulling two rods and reels from the rod box and jamming them into the rod holders, she eased herself behind the wheel of the Ranger bass boat. Flicking a switch, the instantaneous throb of the Mercury engine brought life to the still boat. Pulling the black lever back, the boat responded beautifully and slowly reversed.

The NO WAKE sign bobbed slightly as Jaycee went under the footbridge that connected two of the three peninsulas that comprised the resort area and villas.

Burton Duenke, a realtor from St. Louis, had had the foresight to build the plush resort on the fabulous Missouri lake. Presently Marriott Hotels owned and operated Tan-Tar-A. The Lake of the Ozarks, fed by three rivers, was the largest privately owned lake in the United States. The Union Electric utility company was the original owner. Jaycee's dark eyes scanned the array of private homes and condominiums that snuggled against the lake line. The Army Corps of Engineers rules restricting building within two hundred feet didn't apply on this lake. Docks and piers jutted into the lake. Selfishly Jaycee admitted enjoying the privateness of owning property that edged the lake.

"Best time of the day," Jaycee mumbled, sighing contentedly. The edge of the boat steered unerringly toward the island directly across from the resort area. An underwater reef connecting the island to the mainland was a fisherman's paradise. Trophy-sized large-mouth bass, walleye, crappie, and white bass cohabited the same reef. In early July the white bass were running and the crappie were hitting.

Anchoring the boat twenty yards off the tip of the island gave Jaycee access to the cedar tree crappie bed that only the old timers knew of, and also, with a long cast, she could reach over to the deep side of the reef.

The aquamarine strap, which lifted the cushion of the bench, felt moist with dew as she gripped it. With a tug the seat lifted. She pulled out the hidden tackle box. Weights and sinkers rattled noisily. Unhooking the side latches, she opened the container. A wide array of jigs, still on their display cardboard, were tucked neatly in the bottom of the box. Others were loose, spread colorfully in the top tray.

Jaycee examined each package, searching for a sixteenth of an ounce, chartreuse jig. Finding the lure, she gently removed it from the stapled package.

With the proficiency of years of practice, she tied the miniature jig onto the monofilament line.

"Now, this is living," she said quietly, easing into the chair on the back deck.

Lining herself up with a large sandy brown boulder on the tip of the island, she made a long cast. The lightweight lure made a teeny plunk as it hit the water. Twitching the tip of the graphite rod made the feathered lure resemble the small shad that were the lake's bait fish.

The mist gradually lifted, the sun's rays dissipating its density. Birds began chirping in the large elm trees. Normally Jaycee didn't fish this spot. Skiers loved to circle the island, showing off to admirers on the resort's pavillion, and the wake made by the high powered ski boats had swamped more than one stalwart fisherman.

Jaycee grunted. No skier would be out this early. Skiing was even more dangerous than fishing off this point when the fog was on the lake. Logs and other unseen debris floating in the current of the lake could quickly snap the leg of an unsuspecting skier.

The slightest tap on the line indicated a hungry fish was chasing the lure. Jaycee slowed the twitching jig, giving the predator time to catch its prey. The line tugged.

Flicking the tip of the rod upward, she set the hook.

"White bass," she murmured gleefully as the transparent blue monofilament zigzagged furiously. Ounce for ounce, a white bass fought harder than any other fish in the lake. The fish dove, stripping line from the ultralight rod.

Keep the rod tip up. Let him wear himself out. Don't hog it in. Fishing advice her father had given during early sessions raced through her thoughts.

"Come on, baby. Fish fry tonight," she said coaxingly, as though the fish had ears. Patiently she reeled the fish in. It darted, silver scales sparkling near the surface. A thrill of pleasure made Jaycee chuckle as she saw its size. "Ah, you're a beaut!"

Without benefit of net she hauled the fish in and dumped it into the aerated live well at her feet. The small golden hook popped out of its mouth. Quickly she cast again in the same spot. White bass school. There were more where that one came from. Immediately she felt the tap and set the hook, repeating the action she'd just completed with the first catch.

Jaycee's undivided attention focused on casting, twitching the lure, setting the hook, and getting the white bass into the boat. She didn't notice the fog lifting or hear the drone of ski boats warming up in the marina. The white bass were moving off the tip of the island into the deeper water. Snapping her wrist harder with each cast, Jaycee kept up with the traveling school. Then the sound of an approaching motor finally broke her concentration.

"Oh, no! Oh, my God, no!" Jaycee screamed when she sighted a twenty-foot, high-powered ski boat racing straight at the point. Dropping the rod into its holder, lure still in the water, she began waving and shouting frantically.

32

"Hey! Hey, you stupid imbeciles! Look where you're going."

Her efforts were futile. The driver was watching the skier and she couldn't be heard over the revved-up engines. The blue fiber glass boat headed straight for her!

Jaycee hopped over the seat to the steering wheel. The Ranger's horn blasted. The rapid beeping finally attracted the attention of the ski-boat driver. The boat swirved, cutting its engine.

A collision had been averted, but the huge wake rocked the smaller bass boat precariously. Caught off balance, Jaycee catipulted into the deep water. The last thing she heard was the *zzzzzzit* of line being stripped from her rod.

Opening her eyes under water, she was unable to see through the millions of tiny air bubbles surging toward the surface which were released from her clothing. Jaycee kicked her legs. The dead weight of wet clothes and shoes made the struggle toward air a tortuous battle. What seemed like hours was less than minutes. Black specks floated in front of her eyes, lack of oxygen the cause. Adrenaline pumping, Jaycee made one final thrust up out of the depths.

Gasping for air, she rolled on her back. From the corner of her eye she saw one ski float by. Her chest heaved. Turning her head so that one ear was out of the water, she heard, "Goddamn fisherman. He caught me."

Rolling over, Jaycee used the crawl stroke. The weight of her clothes still a burden, she slowly headed toward the bass boat. With one hand she grasped the ladder at the back of the boat. Shedding her waterlogged deck shoes, she slammed them on the back deck.

"Damn skier," she shouted over her shoulder. "Who sold you the lake!"

Unsnapping and unzipping her jeans, she squirmed and kicked, pulling the sodden heavy mass away from the bikini she wore underneath.

"You damned fool! What were you doing fishing in the middle of the lake?" a male voice yelled back.

"I'm not in the middle of the lake, you arrogant bastard!"

One hand flung the jeans into the boat. Grasping both sides of the ladder, she heaved herself up into the boat. Blue vinyl took on a red cast. Jaycee, shaking from fright, was thrown into a terrible rage when she saw the boat's interior. A rainbow of lures littered the cushions and nylon carpet. It looked like a tool box dropped from a twenty-foot ladder.

"Damn, damn, damn," she muttered angrily. She swung around and shook her fist at the offending boat, which was less than thirty feet away. She stripped off her shirt and flung it over the back chair.

"Hey, you dumb broad. Your hook is sticking in my leg. Come get it out!"

"Dumb broad," she muttered, repeating the insult.

Jaycee considered jerking the butt of the rod. The result would give him something to yell about. Unfortunately she wasn't that hard-hearted.

The skier doing the shouting was being helped into the boat by the attractive young female driver. Jaycee

34

could hear the sympathy gushing. "Poor darling," she heard. "Let me see where you're hurt. She could have killed us fishing there."

"Well, I'll be damned," Jaycee muttered under her breath. "I'm sitting here, minding my own business, a ski boat nearly sinks me, and it's *my* fault!" The litany of events astounded her. Jaycee shifted her weight back and forth, deciding whether to help the skier or not.

"Hey! Hey! Don't do that. You're setting the hook."

Releasing the drag button, Jaycee peeled off several feet, then bit the line off with her small white teeth. She watched the clear, blue-tinged line slither into the water. Grabbing the handle of the automatic anchor, she rotated it over and over, pulling up the twenty-pound weight. With one fluid motion she lowered the trolling motor and bumped the on switch with her big toe. Pressure on the pedal started the small blade twirling. The bass boat edged next to the ski boat.

"Put out your bumpers," Jaycee demanded of the blond Amazon in the bow. "I wouldn't want to scratch my boat on this hunk of junk." The insult was two-edged. The twenty-foot *Mark Twain* was obviously someone's pride and joy, and it was far more expensive than her bass boat.

Clicking off the trolling motor, Jaycee stood and peered into the larger boat. The injured man sat in the bottom hunched over his leg.

"You!" hissed Jaycee, recognizing the blond sun-streaked hair and impressive physique.

"Oh, no," the tax agent mouthed. Rolling his eyes heavenward, he asked, "Why me, Lord? Eighty-seven miles of shoreline and the lady plumber fishes here." He winced, then looked at his leg. "Can you get this harpoon out?"

The small hook was embedded into his muscular calf.

"It's only a little hook. Stop making a big deal out of it. Too bad it isn't a treble hook." Jaycee had pulled enough hooks out of her own hide to know that the pain wasn't nearly as bad as the agent was making it out to be. *Sissy.* "Are you in agony?" she asked sarcastically.

"It's not as bad as being tarred and feathered, but it doesn't match the silver necklace I usually wear," he retorted, as though he'd heard her silent name-calling.

"You know I'm going to have to pop that barbed hook out of there then clip it off, don't you? Maybe you'd rather go to the hospital. They'll give you an anesthetic." The thought of removing the hook was nauseating. It was one thing to take one out of your own finger, but quite another story to be doing it to someone else. Her hands fluttered over her stomach trying to quell the churning.

"Just picture me putting the padlock on your door. You'll love my pain. Do it." The order was curt, brooking no further argument.

Picking the wire snippers up off the bottom of the boat, Jaycee gracefully jumped to the seat of the larger boat.

"Ouuuuch!" Jonathan yelled. "Get off the fishing line!"

Guilt stricken, Jaycee saw the monofilament under her toes and jumped off the seat.

Gray eyes, the color of solder, looked up at her.

"You just succeeded in pulling the barb through. Now cut it off."

Bending down, Jaycee inspected the injury. Short sunbleached hair bristled against the palm of her hand. Rivulets of water made dark streaks as they raced down the muscular male leg. Jaycee snipped off the barb and eased the hook back out the point of entry. Surprisingly there was only a small trickle of blood. Jonathan reclined fully, eyelids closed.

"Has he passed out?" the blonde asked.

"No. But now I know how a fish feels." Remembering his manners, he waved one limp hand from Jaycee to the driver of the boat. "Jaycee Warner, meet my cousin, Kay Wynthrop."

The air was filled with hostility as Kay carefully looked Jaycee over. Self-conscious, Jaycee had the urge to cross her arms defensively over her chest, but squelched it.

The tension and the defiant stance made Kay giggle nervously before saying, "Hard to believe we thought you were a man."

"Your ski beached on the island," Jaycee said, switching the conversation away from herself.

"I'll get it," Kay volunteered, jumping feet first into the lake.

Watching Kay's strong, sure strokes, Jaycee became aware of Jonathan's closeness.

37

"She's a good swimmer," Jaycee said nonchalantly, trying to break the silence. Her heart's tempo increased, as though she were the one retrieving the ski.

Still Jonathan watched her without comment. Silver eyes boldly skimmed over her near-naked body. *You are beautiful,* he telepathed with the glint of silver and a lopsided grin. A step brought him within touching distance.

"I've saved up for twelve hours." One finger trailed across the shoestring tie and small bow at the back of her bikini top. The blue blaze of a torch could not have been hotter. "Will you have dinner with me tonight?"

She shivered as his finger blazed back over the trail. Goosebumps appeared on her arms. Jaycee shook her head. The finger stopped. When she felt the dry ends of her ponytail being used like an artist's brush over the same path, her stomach muscles tightened. Jonathan wound the still-damp, honey-colored hair around his wrist, bringing it over her shoulder. Her own hair betrayed her as it clung to the short golden hairs on his wrist.

"Do you ever wear it down?" He studied the contrast in colors, as though they held the answer to the mystery of the woman who grew them.

"Only at night," Jaycee answered breathily.

"I want to see it loose—it must be beautiful." The tenor voice had grown husky.

Closing her eyes momentarily, she visualized herself with her hair down, in his arms. When she opened them, Jonathan had unwrapped his wrist and was leisurely raking the ends against his cheek. Her fingers itched to stroke the opposite side. Somehow she knew it would have the texture of fine sandpaper. Balling her fingers into a fist at her side, she denied their request. He was getting through to her and she knew it.

"You owe me," he said, pushing the advantage.

"For what?"

"Injuring my leg. The price is dinner and an evening together," he bargained.

"And if I don't pay the price?"

The ends of her hair were turned and rubbed across her cheek like a makeup brush.

"A businesswoman always pays her debts," he answered, flicking the tip over her uptilted nose.

It tickled. A smile spread over her generous mouth.

Jonathan sucked in a deep breath. "That's the first time you've smiled for me," he explained. Her smile was being mirrored by his.

She wondered if his lips could evoke the same pleasure he'd brought by merely touching her back and caressing her hair. Would they be hard and harsh in their masculine demands? Would they seek to suckle at her breasts before even touching her lips? Jaycee shuddered beneath the warmth of his smile as she remembered past encounters, past disappointments.

A coarse laugh passed her lips as she activated her defense mechanism. "Mr. Wynthrop, sue me. As soon as I get out of prison for tax evasion, you can ship me off to debtors' prison."

The thump of a ski against the hull of the boat precluded any further discussion.

"Grab hold," Kay shouted from below, pushing the ski out of the water.

"I'd like to," Jonathan muttered. "Next time I will," he added in a soft, threatening tone toward Jaycee.

"Go take a long walk off a short pier," Jaycee whispered back, unwilling to let him have the last word.

Jonathan pulled the ski into the boat and then he helped his cousin Kay.

"Mission accomplished," Kay said between pants. Blue eyes traveled from Jonathan to Jaycee. The tension between the two was palpable. Kay raked her fingers over short wavy blond hair. "I peeked into your boat. It's a mess. Can we help you straighten up?" she volunteered.

The only thing Jaycee wanted to do was get away from Jonathan. She was drawn to him like solder is to a fitting when heat is applied.

"No, thanks. I'll sort it out." Her rude abruptness was hurled at Jonathan, but hurt Kay. "But thanks for the offer," she added, trying to make amends for unintentionally wounding an innocent bystander.

"Sure thing," Kay responded. "The fireworks are tonight. Are you going to the barbecue and dance?"

"Probably," Jaycee answered. The desire to see Jonathan's reaction was acute. She kept her dark gaze on Kay, denying the desire.

"Good. We'll be there for sure," Kay said with a friendly smile.

Jaycee stepped on the bench seat and swung back into the bass boat. Cautiously, avoiding the hooks spread liberally over the interior, she picked her way back to the driver's seat.

"By the way," Kay began apologetically, "I'm sorry I almost sank you. Jonathan is terrific on skis, but I wasn't watching for fishermen."

Flashing a forgiving smile, Jaycee said in an offhand manner, "I should have been off the point earlier," magnanimously accepting part of the blame. *Where was Jonathan? Had he collapsed in shock at the kindness of her words?*

As if in answer to her unspoken question, a tenor voice rang out, "See you tonight Jaycee, if not before." A promise or a threat?

Not if I see you first, she thought before starting the engine.

Not looking back, Jaycee eased the throttle forward, steering toward a nearby cove. She'd have to get her tackle box in order before zooming to the lake house. Any speed at all would hurl the loose hooks back into her face. Snuggling the boat into the back of the cove, she reached over and pushed the button dropping the rear anchor.

Methodically she began picking up the packages of lures, neatly returning them to the bottom of the tackle box. Picking up the small hooks and sinker was more tedious than repairing leaks in water piping.

Beads of sweat dotted Jaycee's upper lip. The sun had completely burned off the mist and was steadily climbing. Wiping her mouth on the back of her wrist, she tasted the salt. Jonathan was probably still out there skiing his fool head off, she thought, resenting the chore of cleaning up. Women work; men play. There was no justice.

Punching the aerator button on the dashboard, she tried to put all thoughts of the aggravating man from her mind. The small motor whined as it began pumping fresh lake water into the live box.

The muscles in her stooped shoulders began to cramp. Straightening from the kneeling position, she sat back on her heels. Placing her hands at the small of her back, she stretched backward. Order was nearly restored. Only the front deck was still a mess.

The tranquility in the cove was soothing. Taking a break, she eased herself onto the seat, stretched out her legs full length, crossing them at the ankles, and locked her fingers together behind her head. The sun beat down on her face.

She loved the Ozarks. The lake was her think tank. Business problems dissolved when washed in clear lake water. Jaycee frowned. She hoped Jonathan and his family were staying at the hotel. She didn't want the security of her haven invaded on a permanent basis. Her brow relaxed. She hadn't heard about anyone buying a house in the estates. She was safe.

The words *See you later* made her forehead pucker again. No problem, she thought. She'd be with her friends and he'd be with his relatives. It would be easy to avoid him in the throngs of vacationers that came to the fireworks display. She did want to avoid him, didn't she?

Not wanting to pursue that line of thought, she

levered herself up and walked to the front deck. A myriad of tiny feathers, white, green, yellow, and black, clung to the blue carpet. Plucking them out one by one, she restored them to the tackle box tray. Scanning the boat, she made certain she hadn't missed any hooks. She didn't want to find one later . . . in her foot.

The thought of a hook in flesh made the image of Jonathan appear. In swim trunks he looked like a compact, blond god. She remembered the tantalizing fingers touching her sensitized back. Stop it, girl, she admonished herself. Thinking about his virile, athletic body and remembering their mutual attraction could only lead to one thing. T-R-O-U-B-L-E. Thanks to him, she had enough trouble in her professional life. She didn't need to have him messing up her personal life too. She'd keep away from her enemy and stick close to her friends. With that thought in mind, she pulled up the anchor and sped back to her sanctuary.

CHAPTER THREE

"Did you catch anything, or do we get out the silver hook?" Tom shouted over the roar of the engine as Jaycee pulled into the dock.

Cutting the motor, she let the boat drift silently into the open space. Jaycee beamed a broad smile. "No silver hook today!" she answered, giving the thumbs-up sign. She chuckled at the fisherman's joke. If there is no catch, fishermen use the silver in their pockets to buy fish to take home and brag about.

Bouncing down the steps, dark wispy hair flying, blue eyes twinkling, Ruth joined her brother and Jaycee on the dock. "Wait until Jaycee tells you about the one that got away."

"As a matter of fact, I did have a fine specimen hooked," Jaycee quipped. Hoisting the fishing basket that was tied to the dock out of the water, she emptied the white bass out of the live well while telling her audience about the *Homo sapiens* she'd caught and thrown back.

The tale was interspersed with giggles from Ruth and boisterous laughter from Tom. Brother and sister, dear friends that they were, sympathized with the skier.

"Thanks a lot," Jaycee said, dumping the last fish into the basket. "They almost drowned your hostess!"

"Almost counts in horseshoes and hand grenades," Tom retorted. "You know better than to fish that point," he began sternly.

"Okay. Okay," Jaycee sputtered. Her hand rose in a halting motion, stopping the lecture she knew she deserved. "Who's going to help clean the fish?"

"Not I," said Ruth, shuddering at the thought.

"Not I," Tom echoed.

"Same old story. I catch the fish. I clean the fish. You eat the fish." Jaycee sighed dramatically. "Someday I'll eat *all* the fish just like in the 'Little Red Hen'," she threatened with mock ferocity.

"No can do," Tom quipped. "Ruth and I fry the fish and fix the trimmings. The way you cook, you'd be eating them raw," he teased.

"I'm a good cook," Jaycee protested. "Given the right equipment."

"Yeah," Ruth snorted. "A telephone and a fast-food restaurant." The jibe was as friendly as the smile that curved her lips upward.

"Details. Details," Jaycee rejoined. Quickly she changed the subject away from a sensitive point. "What's on the agenda for today?"

Tom flexed his biceps. "I thought we'd go over to the resort pool and I'd give the girls a treat."

Ruth and Jaycee groaned in unison.

Climbing out of the boat, Jaycee swatted Tom on the rump. "Who'd look at an ugly thing like you?"

"Let's see," Tom said thoughfully, then proceeded to tick off a list of female names. "Sara, Lizzy, Nancy, Melanie, Crissy, Joni . . ."

"Come on, lover boy. Let me get the fish stink off and we'll go. Why you'd want to swim in chemically treated water when we could find a nice peaceful cove to swim in beats me."

"No action," Tom replied immediately with a cheeky grin that matched his sister's.

Climbing the native-stone steps up to the cabin, the threesome continued to banter about Tom and his conquests. At twenty-three, he was enjoying playing the field. Over six feet, dark-haired and blue-eyed, the women loved to be squired around town by him. And he loved doing it with all of them.

"Maybe I can find a rich old coot for Ruth and then I'll let my brother-in-law support me in the style to which I'd *like* to become accustomed," Tom cajoled in high spirits.

Punching him playfully in the chest, Ruth retorted, "I'll stick to poor but honest Scotty, thank you." The flicker of a dreamy smile flitted over her plain features.

The mention of the company's CPA made Jaycee's mind skip back to her problems with the IRS. Her smile drooped. *Can't tell Ruth and Tom yet,* she thought. *I don't need to upset them needlessly. It's all a mistake anyway,* she reassured herself. Resolutely she pasted a plastic smile back on her face.

Stepping onto the redwood deck that surrounded

the lake house, Jaycee stopped. Breathing deeply, she filled her lungs with fresh Ozark air. The view in front of her never ceased to thrill her.

"God's country," she heard Ruth murmur.

"That it is," Jaycee agreed solemnly.

The quiet peacefulness was broken by Tom's laughter. "Come on, you Ozark ridge runners. I want to check out some of his finest creations." Hands outlined the curves of an imaginary voluptuous woman.

An hour later Jaycee was stretched out beside an egg-shaped pool, eyes closed. She hovered between being awake and drifting into sleep. The early morning fishing trip plus the intense heat sapped her energy. The clearest of silver-gray eyes intruded behind her eyelids. A blond devil chased her around an empty building partially strung with gleaming copper. Honey-blond hair hung loosely over her back. "Padlock and hasp," she heard her pursuer shout. A wicked chain snaked into her flowing tresses, tugging her scalp.

"Jaycee . . . wake up."

Ruth was pulling the ponytail that hung between their loungers. Eyes fluttering, momentarily disoriented, Jaycee stared into the sun high overhead. Black dots swam in front of the fiery ball.

"You were groaning and twisting as though the hounds of hell were chasing you," Tom commented, bending close. His head blocked the brightness of the sun.

"Not the hounds, their owner," Jaycee said groggily, trying to shake the dream out of her consciousness.

Propping herself up on elbows, she scanned the pool area. The devil she'd dreamed of sat on the far side of the pool by his cousin. Powerful legs dangled into the crystal clear water. Their eyes locked. Silver and copper, binding together just as silver solder melts and flows over copper piping.

Fool, she thought. *The man is trying to close your shop and you're making goo-goo eyes at him.* Her eyes dropped to the tanning lotion in her beach bag. Reaching down, she plucked out the lotion, twisted off the top, and began dribbling it down one slender leg. Protection, that's what she needed. Rubbing the creamy whiteness until it was absorbed into her golden skin, she began the same procedure on the other leg. Not protection from the sun, but protection against a force she knew could be more damaging than ultraviolet rays.

Covertly she glanced through dark, lowered eyelashes across the pool. Jonathan Wynthrop wasn't there. Tom had taken his place next to Kay. Where was he? Deep brown eyes scanned the pool area and spied Jonathan sauntering in her direction.

Handsome, she thought, giving the devil his due. *One of those rare men that looked better with his clothes off than on.* Snug navy trunks clung to lean hips. Each step made masculine thigh muscles flex. Silver-blond hair accented the dark tan.

Conscious of staring once again, she squirted a puddle of lotion between her toes. There was enough for five feet instead of five toes. Aggravated, she swiped the excess fluid off and began rubbing it over her arms and shoulders.

"Ms. Warner . . . may I join you?" The gleam in his eye denied the formal politeness of the request.

Before she could answer, Ruth spoke, "Are you the fish?"

Perplexed by the question, Jonathan lifted an eyebrow.

"The rare species that Jaycee caught and threw back this morning," Ruth explained, flashing the stranger a wide smile.

Tossing his head back, Jonathan laughed heartily. It was a man's laugh, one that rumbled from deep in his chest. "I'm the fish. Unfortunately I wasn't a keeper."

"Oh, I don't know about that," Ruth flirted. "I wouldn't mind keeping you."

Grimacing at her friend, Jaycee asked, "How's your wound, Mr. Wynthrop?"

"Amputation is scheduled for seven in the morning. Want to come and watch?" he teased, lowering himself to the lounger beside Jaycee.

"No, thanks. I'd rather be fishing," she answered. Jaycee hated the huskiness of her voice. Why couldn't she be abrupt . . . rude . . . brittle? She didn't want to be around the man. *Liar,* her heart denied.

"Where did she hook you?" Ruth asked, continuing the conversation.

Jonathan tapped the muscles over his heart. "Here."

Jaycee snortled. Ruth twittered. *Damn the man.*

49

He was making Ruth act like a teenager with overactive hormones.

"The leg," Jaycee spat, clarifying the location of the puncture.

"How dreadful," Ruth gushed, batting her eyes in Jonathan's direction.

The only thing dreadful was watching her friend, who was supposed to be in love with her accountant, drooling over her enemy. Unable to listen to the drivel being exchanged, Jaycee excused herself and dove into the deep end of the pool.

The top of her one-piece suit, upon impact, pulled precariously low. In her hasty departure, she'd forgotten to refasten the strap. Struggling to keep the covering in place, she kicked off the bottom of the pool, clutching the fabric to her chest. Legs fluttering, she propelled herself back to the side. Hooking her elbow over the poolside, she tried to hold the slick, emerald-colored suit up while attempting to rehook the gold clasp. A contortionist would have found the position awkward.

"Ruth!" she called. "Ruth!"

The hairs at the back of her neck lifted as she felt warm fingers trail from her neck over one bare shoulder to her elbow.

"Ruth has gone to get drinks. Can I help?" Jonathan asked the question as he dropped into the water beside her.

Jaycee wanted to let go of the coping, expel the air in her lungs, and sink to the bottom before asking anything from this odious man.

"No, thanks. I'll manage," she replied curtly. All

she had to do was hang on to the side of the pool and her suit, and edge her way around to the shallow end where she could stand. Then both hands would be free to hook her strap.

"Move out of the way," she ordered tartly.

"Please?"

"Please move out of the way," she said, coating politeness with sarcasm.

One long arm wrapped around her narrow waist. Silver eyes twinkled at her predicament. "I'll hold you while you fasten your suit."

The promise was kept. He was holding her. What choice did she have? Their legs tangled together with an intimacy that shocked Jaycee. Had his knee deliberately nudged between her legs? The innocence on his face belied the action. Bringing the strap over her shoulder, she fastened the clip in place.

Icy water on her backside contrasted with the warmth of Jonathan's body. The combination of hot and cold should have produced rain, Jaycee thought, or steam, or a tornado. It was certainly wreaking havoc to her emotional barometer.

"Thank you," she muttered, pulling away.

"Thank you!" Jonathan replied, grinning widely. The innocent look was gone. "It was my pleasure."

Bare inches separated them. The merriment in Jonathan's eyes faded as they dropped to Jaycee's lips. *He's going to kiss me,* she thought. Nervously the tip of her pink tongue licked the chlorinated water from her lower lip. She was given time to refuse. But, tilting her head slightly, she willed him to come closer. She was curious about the taste and

51

feel of his lips. Using her fingertips on the side of the pool, she levered herself upward. Briefly she wondered, would his kiss be gentle? Harsh? Provocative? Demanding?

"Jaycee? Jonathan? Time for liquid refreshment."

The spell that had isolated them from the children laughing and frolicking at the shallow end of the pool was broken. The space between them widened as Jonathan drifted away. She watched him lift himself out of the pool, then turn and offer his hand to her.

Recovery from the magic of the moment was not as swift for her. She wanted to quench her thirst, but not with a Tom Collins. A Jonathan Wynthrop would do nicely. A wry smile crossed her face before she placed her small hand into his. A yank later she was out of the pool, dripping beside Jonathan.

"Later," he promised. With a broad wink he lightly touched her elbow, leading her back to the loungers.

Inwardly Jaycee squirmed. The defenses she'd carefully erected were being blown apart. The force of the physical attraction had to be capped, sealed off. A man, especially a tax agent, wasn't in her blueprint for life.

Sipping the lemony Tom Collins, her eyes strayed to Jonathan. Confidence oozed from each pore more readily than the sweat that glistened on his bronze body. A placid, smug smile twitched the corner of his mouth upward. Jaycee read the smile as anticipation of an easy conquest.

Leaning toward the relaxed male, Jaycee whispered, "In twelve hours you couldn't earn enough to afford me." A triumphant copper-colored gleam entered her dark eyes when his lips thinned into a taut line. Score one for my side, she crowed silently.

One eye opened to a slit. Silver sparks shot toward her. "I can afford any woman who's a T.D."

"T.D?"

"Tax delinquent," Jonathan replied sardonically.

"I've told you . . . the IRS made a mistake!" she hissed through clenched teeth.

"And I've told you . . . we don't make mistakes."

"There's an exception to every rule," she countered, thrusting her jaw forward.

"You're not it," he responded in a bored tone. Stifling a yawn, turning his face away, Jonathan ended the argument.

Fuming, Jaycee faced Ruth. "What's the Cheshire grin for?" she demanded, taking her frustration out on her friend.

"Oh, nothing," Ruth answered loftily.

"Then wipe it off!"

Ruth's grin widened more. Jaycee distinctly heard her suppress a giggle.

"What's so damned funny," she demanded, trying to keep her voice down.

Lying on her side, still grinning, Ruth answered. "You are. That gorgeous hunk of male is heating up your copper heart. The icy shell is melting and dripping under your lounger," she said, pointing to the puddle of pool water. "Kissing in a public pool? Very untypical of Jaycee Warner, lady plumber!" Ruth laughed out loud.

"We weren't kissing," Jaycee denied.

"Tell me another one. Next you'll deny whispering sweet nothings to each other."

"Sweet nothings!" Jaycee exclaimed, sotto voce. Glancing over her shoulder, she checked to see if the object of their discussion was eavesdropping. His eyes were closed. The insufferable know-it-all wasn't listening; he was sleeping!

Jaycee knew this conversation couldn't be continued in a low voice. She wanted to scream and yell her denial. Maybe if she said it loudly enough, often enough, she'd believe it herself.

"I hate him. I hate him. I hate him," she whispered in staccato rapid fire.

"Uh-huh. Sure you do," Ruth replied mockingly. "And pigs fly, giraffes have shells, and cats love water. When I see those happen, I'll believe you." Lowering her oversized sunglasses onto her pert nose, Ruth lay back to absorb the tanning rays of the sun. "That miniature Greek god next to you could whip a bear in the woods with a switch. You've met your match, Jaycee, old buddy."

Standing up, grabbing her towel and beach bag, Jaycee glared from her friend to her enemy. "You're both wrong," she muttered. "I'm going back to the house . . . to clean the fish." The explanation would keep both of them from thinking she was running away. Jaycee never ran from a problem. Why should she start now?

"Mmmmm," Ruth said through closed, upturned lips.

"Aren't you coming?"

"I'll stick around and go back with Tom. You'll

go to the dock and I'll be stuck at the house by myself. I'd rather be here."

"You *could* help with the fish."

"No, thanks. You run along. I'll see you later."

Being dismissed like one of Ruth's first graders was more than Jaycee could take in her present state of mind. Fileting fish wasn't repugnant to her, but it wasn't her idea of fun and games either. The least Ruth could do was keep her company while she did the work. She wouldn't beg though. Stoically she turned to leave.

"Oh, Jaycee," Ruth called sweetly. "Leave the suntan lotion." Twisting her head in Jonathan's direction, she said, "Maybe I'll find . . . someone to put it on my back."

The implication was as clear as the sky overhead— if Jaycee wasn't interested in Jonathan, Ruth was. Biting her tongue, she kept the word *traitor* behind clenched teeth. She should have told Ruth about the IRS incident. Ruth would be coming with her instead of letting the enemy stroke lotion of her back. *Now isn't the time,* she thought. *Not with Big Brother one chair away getting an earful.*

Discretion being the better part of valor, Jaycee tossed the dark bottle on the lounger she'd vacated and headed toward the steps that would lead to the hotel. Flagging a Tan-Tar-A van, she ran over the heated pavement and hopped in.

"One fourteen, please," she instructed the driver.

Minutes later Jaycee stepped off the van at the back of her house. The anger she'd felt earlier dissipated as she compared her lake house with the large old-fashioned brick home in St. Louis. Dark wood, brocades, and crushed velvets formalized the entire effect of her home in the city. At the lake, long windows without drapes faced the water. Leather and natural woven fabrics, blended in earthtones, gave Jaycee a feeling of freedom.

This house was a symbol of her accomplishment. She'd scrimped and saved to buy this slice of heaven. It was hers. A reward for several plumbing jobs well done. She'd earned it. If being "houseproud" was a sin, then she was a devout sinner.

In short order the fish were cleaned and packed on ice. After showering, washing and blow-drying her hair, humming to herself, Jaycee poked around in the kitchen making certain the flour, cornmeal, and pancake mix necessary for the fish fry were stocked. Checking out the interior of the refrigerator, she saw Ruth had prepared the thick creamy tartar sauce. Several bottles of Coke were on the bottom shelf. The sight of her one dietary weakness made Jaycee's throat dry. Not hesitating, she pulled out a Coke from the six-pack and twisted off the top. Chug-a-lugging the dark, cool liquid, she felt the familiar burning sensation at the back of her throat.

"The re-e-eal thing," she gasped appreciatively.

A sharp rap on the back door was the last noise she expected to hear. Tom and Ruth would just walk in. Maybe a neighbor was coming to borrow something. The nearest store was several miles away, so that wasn't uncommon.

Opening the door wide, the welcoming smile

dropped from her face when she saw Jonathan leaning against the door frame.

"Yes, Mr. Wynthrop?" she asked aloofly, not inviting him in.

"I'd like to talk to you for a moment if I may."

"Yes?" she repeated, still blocking the doorway.

"May I come in?" Jonathan asked with pointed
politeness.

"Is this an official visit, Mr. Wynthrop?" she inquired. *He probably wants to appraise the contents
and get ready for the auction,* she thought spitefully.
"This house doesn't belong to Jaycee Plumbing. It's
mine—lock, stock, and fishing dock."

"Unofficial visit, Ms. Warner. Now may I come
in?" There was a grim, determined expression on his
sharp features.

"I'd rather you didn't." She knew he was dangerous. The acceleration of her heartbeat and the tingling she felt along her spine left no doubt as to that
fact.

"Fine. I *courteously* agreed to inform you of the
plans for this evening but . . ." Shrugging his shoulders, he pivoted and began walking away.

"Jonathan . . . wait," she called after him. "What
plans?" Curiosity wouldn't allow her to ignore the
baiting remark. "Oh, hell, come on in."

"Thank you for your gracious offer," he answered
sarcastically. Clearly he was struggling to keep his
temper under control.

Jaycee smelled the woodsy fragrance of his aftershave as he passed through the door. He'd showered
and shaved since she'd left the pool area. His pale

57

blue tennis shorts and matching shirt accented the golden tone of his tan and the clean shine of his sunstreaked hair.

Devastating. She silently admired him. He had the physical attributes of a well-honed construction worker . . . not a pencil pusher.

She was unaware of her own loveliness. Jonathan's gaze traveled from her unbound hair that rippled in gentle waves to her waist, over the pure white silk caftan trimmed with narrow gold cording, to the tiny pink-tipped toes peeping out of golden high-heeled sandals.

The electrical charge passing between them scorched the molecules of antagonism into oblivion. It transcended beyond anger. Beyond words that would hurt. The attraction was on a higher level . . . far from the banalities of the everyday world.

As water is drawn downhill by the force of gravity, such was the force moving Jonathan toward Jaycee. Gray eyes bright as newly minted dimes, sought the mysteries hidden in her dark copper-flecked ones.

With infinite gentleness, Jonathan enclosed Jaycee against him. She felt the sensuous warmth of his hands brushing over her hair, stroking the silky fabric against her bare skin. How had he known her back was the most exquisite of her erogenous zones?

Lips tucked beneath his chin explored the tanned skin over the pulse that had begun to beat faster. Slender arms entwined around his neck.

"Truce, Jaycee?" he asked hoarsely. Circles drawn by his fingertips increased then decreased in size.

"Peace," she answered. She couldn't fight the

inevitable. Didn't want to. It felt right being in his arms.

Jonathan softly brushed his lips against her forehead. A kiss? Leaning back in the cradle of his arms, she watched for a triumphant smile. There was none. The fullness of his lips was rewarded by the cool softness of her own mouth. The hands at her back trembled, but continued their enticing path.

Until Jonathan, no man had restrained himself. Or was it only boys she'd had physical encounters with? Did he know that the elongated circles that raked from shoulder blade to narrow hips were shooting fires below their touch?

"Kiss me?" She'd never asked before. Curiosity had to be satisfied.

Jaycee wasn't prepared for the explosion that occurred. His lips fused and sealed over hers. Behind closed lids the Fourth of July fireworks had begun ahead of schedule. She'd read about rockets bursting, throwing balls of fire through the bloodstream, but thought it poppycock. It wasn't. Multicolored bursts ignited a passion that brought a primeval groan from her soul.

The kiss deepened. Jonathan tasted the honey in the uncharted recesses of her mouth. She arched against him when the strength of his palms rotated low on her back.

"This is crazy," he murmured raggedly, breathing deeply, as if their kiss had seared his lungs.

"Then take me to Farmington," she whispered, mentioning the location of the state mental hospital. "Only if we can reserve adjoining rooms. I'll never have enough of this," he murmured against her lips before reclaiming them.

Hands entwined in the long length of hair. The fireworks began again for Jaycee. Using the breadth of his shoulders, she pulled him closer. Her torso flattened against the muscular wall of his chest. Twin mounds of flesh hardened. Tips became erect.

Neither heard the back door open nor saw the flabbergasted expression on Tom's face. Before he could think, the words *What's up?* were out of his mouth.

Jonathan groaned, breaking the kiss, but not the embrace. Lowering her arms to rest lightly on Jonathan's biceps, she heard him mutter, "Me." The flush on her cheeks deepened when she caught the explicit meaning.

An embarrassed laugh slipped between her lips while she struggled to regain her own composure.

"Tom," she said, without looking at him, "your timing is lousy. Be a pal and fix us all a drink."

Laughing boyishly at her criticism, Tom went into the small kitchen. Jaycee could hear him loudly banging bottles around to let them know they were alone again.

"Sorry about that," Jonathan mumbled, backing away.

Jaycee turned a ramrod stiff back toward him. Pride lifted her chin. *An apology for a kiss. How humiliating.* Unexpected girlish tears threatened to spill out of her eyes as a lump blocked her throat. Abruptly she felt herself twirled around to face Jonathan.

"My God, you're sensitive," he said softly. "I was apologizing for my uncontrollable *overt* reaction."

"Can I come in now?" Tom shouted from the kitchen.

"Not yet," Jonathan replied gruffly.

The smile she beamed up at him was like the sun bursting through heavy nimbus clouds.

"Okay now?" he asked.

Jaycee nodded her head. Gravity caused one tear to dislodge. Before she could wipe it away with the back of her hand, Jonathan removed it with a kiss.

"Your tears even taste good," he teased. "Just the right amount of salt to balance"—swiftly he brushed a kiss on her mouth—"the sweetness of your lips."

"How about the acidity of my tongue?" Unaccustomed to compliments, she covered her flustered emotions with caustic words.

"Passion neutralizes the acid factor," he answered, giving her an understanding hug.

"Now?" Tom called. "Your drinks are getting watery."

"Now!" the occupants of the living room chorused.

The cherubic smile of an angel was smeared on Tom's face when he brought three beers, each in a frosty mug, into the living room.

Jonathan's eyebrow cocked. "How does beer get watery?"

The glass mugs clinked together on the coffee table when Tom put them down.

"Would you believe . . ." Tom began imitating the

old television program Don Adams starred in as Agent 86.

"No, we would not," Jaycee responded, laughing.

The embarrassment of being caught in a compromising position was removed by Tom's comic relief. Jaycee seated herself on the sofa, tucking her slender legs beneath the flowing caftan. Patting the cushion, she silently invited Jonathan to sit beside her. He smiled, seated himself, and draped one arm over her shoulders.

"Did you tell her?" Tom asked.

Jonathan's arm stiffened. A threatening silence invaded the room. Jaycee had a gut-level feeling that she wasn't going to like what she was about to hear.

"Not yet," Jonathan said tersely.

Tom mouthed a vulgar expletive. "If you'll excuse me, I'm going to the bedroom. I seem to have contracted a severe case of hoof-and-mouth disease."

"I'm hoping it's fatal," Jonathan responded.

Waiting for the unknown was worse than knowing. The daggers shooting from Jonathan toward Tom left no doubt in Jaycee's mind that she was about to be hurt. When he removed his arm and braced his elbows on spread knees with the beer mug between his hands, she knew the blow was coming.

"Ruth arranged for all of us to go to the festivities tonight together," Tom began quietly. The tension increased.

Jonathan's eyes focused on the minuscule bubbles soaring from the bottom of the beer mug. Softly he said, "Ruth is my date."

CHAPTER FOUR

Direct hit. Right below the belt. Jaycee turned her face toward the patio doors overlooking the lake. Four words had spoiled the rapture they had shared.

"Tom, we're going out on the sundeck, and no one is to disturb us." Jonathan's thumb and forefinger formed a manacle around her wrist. "I'm not leaving until this is straightened out," he said, the force of his voice equal to the pressure exerted as he pulled Jaycee up from the sofa.

Using a defensive tactic she had been taught in a karate class, she freed her arm. "Force won't work," she spat out. "As far as I'm concerned, there is nothing to straighten out. Ruth is your date. Period." It didn't take a college degree to decipher his intentions. Jonathan was older than Tom, but obviously his male ego needed a strong support system. Fast as he worked, he'd leave and have another woman waiting for a midnight date, she thought glumly.

"If you prefer to have Tom referee, I won't object. However, I think it only fair to warn you—we won't be discussing the plans for this evening *exclusively*," he threatened with a low, silky smooth voice.

It galled her to be manipulated. Shrewd, callous, unscrupulous, were a few names she'd like to call Jonathan. Those were the nice adjectives. The foul names were unlimited. He had the upper hand and was wielding it with force. Unless she wanted Tom to know where she had first met Jonathan, and the circumstances of the meeting, she had to agree to a private discussion.

Jonathan strode to the sundeck door, opened it, and motioned for her to follow. Dark eyes narrowing, sparks flying, she traced his footsteps. "Despicable lout," she muttered when she passed in front of him.

Leaning over the bannister of the deck, she avoided his mesmerizing eyes. The hairs at the back of her neck lifted of their own accord as he stood behind her.

"I'm perpetually out of step with you," he began, placing strong hands loosely on her shoulders. "I'm either moving too quickly, or lagging behind. But I'm trying to march to your beat." Gently he turned Jaycee around, lifting her chin with one crooked finger. "We were synchronized in there a few minutes ago."

Jaycee hardened herself against the persuasive talk. Stiffening her arms, clenching her fists, short nails digging into the palms of her hands, she blocked the warmth his words evoked.

"Fifteen minutes after you left the pool, Ruth devised a scheme that would bring Scott to his knees."

"Aren't you a little old for games?" Jaycee asked with ridicule in her voice.

"My exact words to Ruth," Jonathan answered. A satisfied smile appeared on his lips. "In the next ten minutes she had me convinced her entire love life was in my 'capable' hands."

"Rather egotistical of you to agree, wasn't it?"

Jonathan ignored the verbal jab. "But the whole time she talked there was one thought in my mind: I won't see Jaycee on a social basis again unless I play a part in Ruth's scheme. You would avoid me at all costs. Right?"

She didn't reply.

"Sooooo," he said, drawing out the vowel sound, "I took a chance. I agreed to be Ruth's escort *if* I could tell you the truth beforehand. We have enough problems in the background without having misunderstandings or playing games."

"Is that why you came over? To tell me you were participating in one of Ruth's first-grade games?" Harsh laughter filled with scorn coursed from Jaycee's mouth. "That's pitiful, Jonathan."

A hard glint came into his eyes. "Yes, it is. The only thing more pitiful is a warm, passionate woman refusing to trust me because she's afraid."

"I'm not afraid of you," she lied.

"You are, and we both know it," he said firmly. "I've tried everything to break through your barriers. The minute I get close you slap up another one. A few minutes ago they cracked. Now you're trying to mend them." Jonathan pulled Jaycee against him. "I've seen how you try to laugh away an emotional moment, or use your sharp tongue. Please, don't do

65

that with me anymore, Jaycee." His voice became softer, gentler.

Tenderly he draped his arms over her slender shoulders and cascading hair. Jaycee tilted her head until their eyes met. The deep sincerity she saw wrenched her heart. For the first time in years she wanted to trust. Tentatively, unsure of herself in this situation, she laid her head against the soft blue cotton covering his chest.

"I can't promise not to laugh in your face or cut you down. The barriers you spoke of are all the protection I have." Sensuous fingertips thread into the hair at the nape of her neck. Her scalp tingled when they found the valley at the base of her skull. The captured nerve center sent sweet messages throughout her relaxed body. A fragile piece of Steuben glass couldn't be held with more care.

"Give what we have a chance. Hmmm?" Jaycee's drawn-out question made Jonathan's chest hum against her cheek.

Nodding her head, Jaycee asked, "What about tonight?"

"Tonight? Ruth will be my date, but I'll be thinking of you. The attention I'll shower on her will be what I want to expend on you." His arms tightened, drawing her closer. "With any luck at all, we'll steal away into the night and let them solve their own problems."

Without wasting further time, motion, or words, he bent and tenderly kissed her. The intimacy of their sealed lips was satisfying. It meant as much to her as the questing, exploring kiss they had shared earlier. His lips trailed over her cheek, leaving a warm, moist path. He swept her hair aside, his small kisses blazing a trail to the back of her neck.

"Your hair smells like sunshine," he mumbled near her shell-like ear. "This morning I knew I wanted to bury my face in it. Lose myself in its softness."

Moving his open collar aside, placing a kiss in the shadowed V of his collar bone, she listened, loving what she was hearing. The silky caftan was being blown around his legs, its whispering softness holding them together. Strains of honey-blond hair, like a golden web, mingled with his lighter hair as the breeze caught the shining threads. Small noises came from the back of her throat. They were close . . . so close.

Lowering the barriers was exciting and scary. Letting Jonathan behind them could be dangerous, but the blood throbbing, racing, through her veins ignored the danger.

"Jonathan . . . oh, Jonathan. You're making me dizzy. We're going too fast," she whispered into the pulse beating rapidly on his throat.

Hugging her soundly, placing one sharp nibble on her earlobe, he drew away. Short breaths fanned her face. Unable to deny himself, he swiftly gave her a hard kiss, then stepped backward.

"That isn't enough. I want much more of you. But . . . we'll take it slowly."

Jaycee could have uttered the same words. That was exactly how she felt. They had to be cautious of the chemistry that swept through them when they touched.

"What time are we all going out tonight?" She couldn't force herself to say, "When are you picking Ruth up?" She didn't want to be any part of Ruth's game.

"Dinner at eight. Ruth invited Kay and myself over for a before-dinner drink."

"That's when Scotty gets the surprise treatment?" False gaiety made her voice rise higher than normal. The wayward strands of hair kept blowing toward his face. Impatiently she caught them with one hand, tucking them behind one ear.

Jonathan caught her fingers. Silver eyes sent a message she couldn't decode until he raised her open palm to his lips and traced her love line with the tip of his tongue. "Don't create a problem where there doesn't need to be one," he said softly when he turned the back of her hand against his cheek. Lightly he drew it from his cheekbone to chin. The soft sandpaper texture was as she had earlier thought it would be.

"I'll try not to," she answered solemnly.

"I'd better go before I feel the need to convince you again." A broad smile split his generous lips. "Come, walk me to the door, then I'll have an excuse to kiss you again." When he tucked her hand into the crook of his arm, she gently squeezed the hard flesh.

"You need an excuse to kiss me," she teased, glancing at him through lowered lids.

"Not an excuse . . . an opportunity," he bantered.

"An opportunist, eh, Mr. Wynthrop?" she asked as they proceeded toward the door.

"I'm telling you I want to kiss you again," he answered, still grinning.

Moments later he did. A brief departure kiss that managed to shake the floor beneath her feet. She watched his loose-limbed gait as he climbed the path to the paved street. The happy whistling she heard, though a different tune, was the same song her heart sang.

Closing the door, she felt like clapping her hands and shouting her happiness. Her spirits were soaring. Only Jonathan had made that happen. Tonight was going to be special, she thought, before remembering Ruth's plot. As she twirled in place, her long hair and silky caftan making a wide, graceful arch, she decided to tolerate the plan. When Jonathan complimented Ruth, she'd close her eyes and pretend he had said it to her.

The door behind her opened. Ruth walked in, lugging a beach bag, an oversized towel, and a flotation device. Perspiration coursed down her cheeks.

"Scotty isn't here yet, is he?" she asked before collapsing on the leather love seat. She relieved her burden by dumping it beside the coffee table.

"You mean, dear Scotty . . . the man you *supposedly* love?" Jaycee asked with sweet sarcasm.

"Uh-oh. You don't like my scheme." Dragging the end of her towel off the floor, Ruth wiped her face on one corner.

"In a word? No," Jaycee said succinctly.

"I knew you would never go along with it unless I roped Jonathan in on it first."

"Perceptive, dear friend. Very perceptive." Jaycee

sat down on the matching leather couch catty-corner from Ruth. "Fill me in on the gory details." The demand was spoken in a subdued tone, but the copper beneath the velvet was evident.

"After you left, I decided that lovable but aloof Scotty needed to have a serious fishing lesson." Blue eyes gleamed brightly.

"Only you could equate fishing lessons with love. Explain," Jaycee coaxed, not catching the mysterious analogy.

"Scotty doesn't realize he isn't the only fish in the ocean." Spreading the damp terry cloth towel over her bare legs, she absentmindedly pulled at a loose thread. "*You've* told me a thousand times," she exaggerated, "that he loves me. I'm yet to hear it from him." The thread snapped, making a tiny hole.

"So," Jaycee answered, "you're going to cuddle up to Jonathan, hoping the green-eyed monster will tow Scotty begging and pleading into your arms."

"He doesn't have to beg. I'd prefer 'passionately into my arms,' " Ruth amended, a happy lilt in her voice.

"It won't work."

"What do you mean, it won't work?" Ruth demanded, flinging the towel off her lap.

"Scotty doesn't have a jealous bone in his body. This is an old trick that won't work," she explained. "And, frankly, I don't want to be a part of it."

Ruth slumped back on the sofa, folding her arms across her chest. "There are other *older* tricks I could have tried." A mild threat hung in the air between the two women.

70

"Pregnancy?" Jaycee queried with a scoff. "I can see you explaining *that* to the school board." Ruth might want her MRS. degree, but she wouldn't endanger her career.

"Wouldn't you rather go along with my folly tonight than take a chance of my turning up jobless and pregnant on your doorstep," Ruth wheedled.

Jaycee roared with laughter. Swallowing the wrong way, she went into a coughing spasm. Ruth quickly crossed over and pounded Jaycee unmercifully on the back.

Fending off her friend with one arm, Jaycee gulped, clearing a breathing passage.

When the coughing ceased and Jaycee's face returned to its normal color, Ruth demanded, "What's so funny?"

"You sound just like you did when we were kids on the playground and you tried to convince me to give you the homemade pie out of my lunch," Jaycee answered, chuckling softly.

A perky smile lit Ruth's face. "If I remember correctly, you gave me the pie."

"Yeah. But you had to promise to be my best friend forever."

A knowing smile passed between the two women. Ruth had been her best friend. But no stretch of the imagination could place Scotty in the same category as a piece of pie. He couldn't be divvied up that easily. Resigned to the inevitable, Jaycee shook her head.

"All right. Take the pie."

Ruth hugged Jaycee smiling with delight.

71

"But don't blame me if it doesn't work," Jaycee warned.

"I won't," Ruth reassured her. "You know," she said thoughtfully, "you and Jonanthan have a lot in common. He screamed and kicked too, then capitulated when I least expected it." A questioning look passed from Ruth to Jaycee.

Loftily Jaycee said, "We're mature, intelligent adults who don't play games."

The superior smile drooped when Ruth said, "Love *is* a game."

"I hope you are wrong," she muttered quietly. "I've always been a nonparticipant, remember?"

Ruth must have realized her blunder. "New game . . . new rules. Don't let those old insecurities rise to the top. Pardon the pun," she teased, trying to bring the smile back to Jaycee's face.

Unfolding herself and rising from the couch, Ruth picked up her swimming paraphernalia and said, "I'm going to avail myself of the plumbing wonders and take a shower." Turning back toward Jaycee, she added, "I like Jonathan. You can trust him."

"I do," Jaycee replied, the broad smile having returned. "Don't pour it on too thick tonight, huh, friend?"

Ruth returned the smile with a hint of mischief and headed down the steps, clunking her beachbag on each step.

Jaycee gathered the mugs, took them into the kitchen, and loaded them into the half-filled dishwasher. Bracing her arms against the sink, she stared at the arrow-leaf philodendron swaying from the current of air coming from the air conditioner. The swaying green plant mesmerized Jaycee into total stillness. Was love a game where the participants manipulated each other? she asked herself. Did this undefinable yearning she had every time Jonathan touched her qualify her as a player? Was he an experienced gamester moving her from emotion to emotion, without her being aware?

The memory of their embrace made her breasts tighten, nipples peaking. She wondered if his hands would cup and stroke them. Locked in her daydream, she could almost feel his tongue circling, sipping, bringing the mounds to life. The wanting ache began throbbing as she visualized his sunbleached head nestled in the valley of her breasts. Her hand touched the cleavage, fanned over the small rib cage to her navel, across the firm muscles of her abdomen. She revelled in the fantasy of Jonathan's hands stroking, arching her toward him. It was real. Beautiful. Not a game.

The sound of the doorbell snapped Jaycee's eyes open. The dream was gone. The cool stainless steel sink raked a straight line just below her ribs, creasing the fabric of her caftan. Hastily, somewhat guilty over the sexual fantasy, she moved to the door. The bell rang again.

"Scotty! Come in," she welcomed him.

"Thanks." The rounded, cherubic pink face beamed a jolly smile at his friend, client, and hostess for the weekend. "Phew, it's hot out there." He set his suitcase down, stuck his fishing rods in the umbrella stand, withdrew a handkerchief from his back pocket, and began mopping his forehead. His medium height and rotund build went nicely with his chubby face and slightly receding hairline. "This air conditioning feels terrific. Are the others here?"

"Mmmm-hmmm. They came in last night."

Tucking the damp handkerchef in his back pocket, he shouted past Jaycee, "Tom! Ruth! I'm here."

Minutes later they were convivially exchanging hugs, handshakes, and conversation. Jaycee smiled at Ruth's enthusiastic embrace. How could she make Scotty think she was falling for another man after a greeting like that, Jaycee mused, chuckling to herself. Scotty will see through her plan in a minute unless he's blind.

"Hey, ol' man, you'd better haul that stuff downstairs and get ready," Tom said after glancing at the clock on the mantel.

"Ol' man?" Scotty gasped. "You could build a few muscles yourself," he jibed, "carrying those suitcases downstairs." He tried to convince Tom that toting luggage would be more fun than whitewashing a picket fence.

"Okay, Mark Twain, I'll carry the suitcase. You'll need your strength just to change clothes and shower," Tom quipped.

"Ruth, you're going to have to teach that *boy* respect," he complained in a mockingly serious tone.

"That *boy* has a terrific blonde lined up for tonight. And wait until you see my date!"

"I'll see him downstairs in the mirror when I shave," Scotty chuckled. "Your zeal is justified. I am a handsome brute," he said jokingly. Being anything

74

other than good-looking didn't bother Scotty. His warm personality made him well liked by everyone.

"*My* date won't be in front of the mirror downstairs," Ruth stated, enjoying the surprised expression on Scotty's face. "He'll be here shortly. He's absolutely scrumptious!" Ruth rolled her eyes like a teenager at a rock concert.

Jaycee shrugged her shoulders when Scotty shot her a questioning glance.

"Well, my blond angel. It's you and me, babe." Grabbing Jaycee, he swung her off the floor and twirled her around. Noisily he placed a big kiss on her cheek. "I'll make this a night you'll remember."

Ruth couldn't see the steely glint in the twinkling blue eyes that Jaycee did. "Put me down, you fool," Jaycee gasped, breathless from the rambunctious swinging.

The game had a new twist. One Ruth hadn't planned on. Scotty refused to be sucked into a jealous rage. Ruth had lost before the game had even started.

"Sweetheart," he said softly, "I'm going to show you an evening you'll never forget." The words were spoken to Jaycee, but the meaning behind them was for Ruth.

CHAPTER FIVE

The plan was a disaster—from the introductions to drinks, to dinner. Kay and Tom had made a hasty exit. Jaycee, Scotty, Jonathan, and Ruth sat in silence on the wooden pavilion facing the island, waiting for the fireworks display to begin.

Jaycee was disgruntled with the whole misspent evening. Over drinks she had listened to Jonathan compliment Ruth on her hair, her slender figure, and her sundress. It made Jaycee, who was dressed in a one-piece red culotte ensemble, feel like a Coke machine. For a quarter she'd dispense a can of poison to Scott, Ruth *and* Jonathan. This was no love game. It was total war. Nuclear holocaust couldn't be more destructive.

The cocktail party was bad; dinner was worse. Scott had actually cut her meat into small bite-size pieces and lovingly fed her. Keeping his eyes constantly on her, he'd smile, wink, pat her hand, and worst of all . . . whisper in her ear. Putting her hand to the side of her mouth, blocking Ruth and Jonathan's view, she explicitly told him to cut it out. Clucking her under the chin, Scott told her not to whisper sweet nothings in front of guests. He was having the time of his life. Everyone else was miserable.

Silver eyes took on a greenish tint. Did Jonathan think she enjoyed being fawned over? Scotty was too busy babying her to notice the hand draped over Ruth's shoulder or the nibbling kisses Ruth pasted on Jonathan. Their efforts dwindled; Scotty's flourished. Jaycee cringed.

"Baby doll, if we wanted to get to the other side of the lake," Scotty enthused, "we could walk across by hopping from boat to boat."

"Go fall in the lake and drown," she heard Ruth, who was sitting next to her, mutter. Jonathan, on the other side of Ruth, was ominously silent.

When Scotty picked up her hand and kissed each oval fingernail, Jaycee groaned. Ruth and Jonathan glared.

"I love your sweet moans of passion," Scotty said.

Leaning forward, Scotty asked Ruth, "Had enough, babe? Or shall we continue this farce all evening?"

Before Ruth could, Jaycee answered, "*I've* had enough." Turning toward Ruth and standing, she demanded, "More over."

Silently they exchanged places.

"Bravo," Jonathan murmured into her ear. "If you'll excuse us," he said, leaning past Jaycee toward the other couple, "we're going to stroll around the paths until the fireworks start." Lacing Jaycee's fingers between his, he didn't wait for a reply.

Minutes later they were on a dark path edging the

lake. Jonathan's purposeful stride had Jaycee practically trotting at his side. Rebelling at the cavalier treatment, she dug in her heels, tugging at the long fingers imprisoning her hand.

"Are we trying out for the Olympics?" she asked sarcastically. One hard jerk freed her hand.

Jonathan snorted, continuing on into the darkness. With a burst of speed she passed him and physically blocked his strides. "Well?" she demanded. "What's the problem?"

"You," he answered curtly, sidestepping off the path.

"Me?"

Head bent, he went on at a brisker pace. Long steps lengthened the gap between them. "Let me walk off my hostitlity, will you?" he said over his shoulder.

Jaycee stopped in her tracks. "Hostility?" she echoed quietly in a bewildered tone. *He clamors all over Ruth and now he's angry,* she silently fumed. They make the basic rules for the game, Scott twists them, and she has to tolerate a runaway player?

"Jonathan," she called loudly toward the top of the hill. "I'm going back. The fireworks are about to start."

"Don't." The negative order stayed her leaving.

A familiar tensing in the muscle of her right leg was the only thing stopping a headlong retreat. "Damn," she muttered. "Why can't I be like other people and get tension headaches," she complained, willing her big toe to stay flat. Quickly sitting, her left leg stretched out, right leg bent to her chest, she

78

massaged the bunched muscle. The big toe lifted a fraction of an inch. Groaning, Jaycee kneaded harder. "Great! Just great!"

Heavy footfalls behind her signaled Jonathan's return. Jaycee grimaced at him. The knot in her leg tightened.

Hunkering to his knees, he asked, "Charley horse?"

Shaking her head, she answered behind clenched teeth, "My version of a migraine."

Pushing her hand aside, he deftly began kneading from ankle to knee, using both hands. Slowly she saw her big toe relaxing. The calf muscle began to loosen, becoming flaccid.

"Do you have these often?"

The aftereffect, a pain like a thousand prickling needles, made her suck in her breath. This sensation was more intense than having a foot fall asleep, become numb, then awaken.

Finally the prickling eased. "Not since I was a teenager."

Jonathan's head rose. Concern made parallel lines stretch over his forehead. "Better?"

"Gone, but not forgotten. And you?"

"The same." Bending forward, he kissed her kneecap. "Ruth's game nearly earned Scotty a prize punch in the mouth," he stated grimly. He sat back on his heels, glaring at Jaycee.

"A plunger," Jaycee disagreed, laughing. "One more bite of food and I'd have smacked him with a plumber's friend." Her musical laughter increased as she visualized the threat.

"You loved it." Jonathan wasn't laughing. "You whispered sweet nothings in between bites," he accused her.

Jaycee laughed harder. She tucked the culottes under her knees and drew her legs up to her chest. "You and Ruth were as thick as icing on a cake, and Scotty ignored it." Giving Jonathan a rueful smile, she asked, "Jealous?"

"A little," he admitted begrudgingly. A slight smile tilted his mouth upward. He moved beside her on the path. "And you?" It was the same question she had asked earlier.

Dodging the question, she murmured, "People are jealous when they . . . care."

"I care," he said softly.

"A little?"

Pressing the palm of her hand to his mouth, his lips caused a pleasurable tingling as they moved, saying, "Want to find out how little? Or how much?" His teeth nipped the flesh below her thumb.

"I'm a Missourian. Show me." The state motto flowed glibly over her dry tongue.

Stretching her fingers out, he kissed the last knuckle on each finger. A delicious feeling of anticipation made her lips part, her eyes close. Turning her hand over, he kissed the corresponding bend.

"How do you feel about being passionately ravaged here and now?"

"Same answer."

"Lady . . ."

Jaycee could sense his gaze on her face. Lazily lifting her lids, copper fires began glowing. Invitingly

80

she leaned back on her elbows. Tiny pebbles poked into her skin. She didn't notice. All powers of concentration were on the silver lights defying the darkness as they came closer and closer.

"Lady . . ." The single word was softly, almost wistfully spoken.

The velvety black sky overhead shattered into glorious sparks of fire. The boom of the first test rocket ricocheted over the silent hills.

". . . come on." In one fluid motion he was on his feet. A tremor ran through the hand extended toward Jaycee.

Standing beside him, disappointment extinguished the copper flames in her eyes.

"Does your leg hurt?" he asked when she limped a step or two.

"Want to kiss the pain away?" she asked beguilingly.

Hesitating, Johnathan seemed torn in two directions. "Jaycee, I promised myself that if you started to trust me, I would not do anything to hurt you." One hand raked through his hair as he thrust the other into his pants pocket. "We're on this hillside because I was in danger of exploding with frustration down there. When I walked away, it was to keep myself from brutalizing your mouth with kisses. You didn't deserve that reaction, but don't entice me now. My emotions are raw." One arm pulled her against the hardness of his chest. "I want to kiss *all* the pain away. Yours and mine."

Acknowledging his dilemma, she raised herself on tiptoes and gently covered her lips with her own. She

81

invited the kiss to deepen by pressing her hands into the soft short hair above his collar. His tongue and teeth sipped and tugged sweetly on her lower lip, requesting entry into the privacy of her mouth. Her lips slowly parted. He rotated, swirled, and gradually thrust himself into her deeply. A kittenish purr came from the back of her throat. He sought and found each darkened crevice. The effect was devastating.

She didn't know whether more test rockets were being fired, or if the pounding of her heart was making that thunderous noise. The tension that had caused the pain in her leg dissipated like flux put on hot copper. She pressed closer to the source of heat. Spreading his legs, shifting his weight, he steadied the embrace. Closely held, the buckle of his belt pinched her waist when he hungrily consumed all she offered. Trembling from her unleashed passion, she felt Jonathan drawing away. Sealing her lips by running the rigid point of his tongue at the crevice of her lips, he asked huskily, "Scared?"

"To death."

"Of me?"

"Of myself," she answered shakily.

"Why?" her murmured, gently kissing her neck.

Knowing she was scared and knowing why she was scared were two different things. Living in the twentieth century she had some experience as to where the desire she felt led. She wasn't afraid of sex. She was afraid it would be less than what she wanted. Was being in love the secret ingredient missing in other encounters?

Jonathan had said he cared. Caring was part of

loving. His tongue circled her ear, stopping to nibble on the lobe, then darted in and out. Jaycee was too distracted to think. He was wreaking havoc on all her senses. His question went unanswered under his onslaught. Logic, rationality, practicality, were tossed into the summer's breeze.

"I want you, love," she heard murmured into her ear. Held closely to his hips, she understood his need. If he wanted her, needed her, cared for her . . . wasn't that enough? The ache deep inside her didn't ask for more.

"A little?" she whispered against his neck.

Jaycee had to ask. Find out if his need was greater than the caring he had earlier professed. If one was less than the other, sex would merely be a romp in bed. She didn't need physical release of that sort.

Hands kept sliding from shoulder blades to hips, but his lips halted. She held her breath, waiting for the answer.

"When you're in my arms, I want you badly," he confessed honestly. "When I'm away from you, I find it hard to concentrate because you're always in the back of my mind. At thirty-four I've certainly experienced wanting a woman, but *never* have I had to pry one out of my mind to get my work done. You're a totally unknown phenomenon." He wound a loose tendril of her hair around his finger. "I really don't know if that is love . . . but it's way ahead of anything I've ever felt before."

The air in her lungs gradually dispelled itself. The truth hadn't answered all of her questions, but his honesty, even though his stiff manhood surged against her, was refreshing. In the throes of desire most men would have declared their love and rushed her to the nearest bed. Love at first sight was beyond her realm of comprehension also. A man and woman could be attracted to each other, as they were, but that wasn't love. Not the kind that lasted a lifetime.

"I've never been in love either," she said, baring her own soul. "Sexually curious, but"—she searched for the right words—"never fulfilled."

"Since you haven't been in a convent, I would hardly expect the normal curiosity of a woman not to include sex," he said, dismissing virginity as being unimportant. Backing slightly away he took her hand and began walking slowly to the pavilion. "When we make love, I want it to be perfect for you. No hustle. No frantic coupling. You mean more to me than that."

"You sound awfully confident," she said, his words heightening the expectation she already felt.

Smiling down at her, he replied, "I am. Unless I'm misconstruing all the signals your luscious body is sending, you want me too. Maybe not tonight or tomorrow, but sometime in the near future."

The fireworks distracted them from further conversation. The incline leveled off as they neared the pavilion. Talking and being heard was impossible the closer they came.

Jonathan nuzzled her neck. "We'll make plans when the fireworks are over."

Weaving their way through the crowd, they returned to their seats next to Ruth and Scotty. Her friends beamed a smile toward her. Jonathan squeezed her hand. The next half-hour was spent oohing and ahhhing over the heavenly display. The ground fireworks lit up the whole island with a replica of the American flag.

Jaycee could feel goosebumps rise on her arms when the loudspeakers began playing the national anthem. Everyone respectfully stood. The glow of the display lasted until the final strains of the music ended. With a mighty swish a multitude of rockets shot into the air simultaneously. The stars were blocked from view as they began exploding against the darkened sky. White, green, blue, red, green, purple, orange—all blending, shattering, spreading, popping, until they filled the sky. Spontaneously horns hooted on the lake. The audience clapped showing its appreciation. The climax was stupendous.

Japanese lanterns strung along the edge of the decking flickered on. At the back of the pavilion a dance band began playing a popular country-western melody. Small tables were being brought into the seating area. Shortly a table and chairs were provided for the foursome.

When the waiter requested their order, Scotty stood and shouted it over the loud music. Jaycee noticed Ruth scratching and rubbing her face. Nose, chin, forehead, eyebrows, ears—like a dog with a colony of fleas. *What in the world is wrong with her?* Jaycee thought. *Had the misfired game made her break out in hives?* She appeared to have gotten over being piqued when she and Jonathan had joined them.

Grabbing her wrist, Jaycee shook her head. Using sign language, she tried to make Ruth stop the scratching. The volume of the outdoor speakers slackened as someone adjusted them.

"Stop scratching," Jaycee commanded.

Ruth held her hand directly in front of Jaycee's dark eyes. A bright diamond twinkled on her fourth finger.

"Ruth! Congratulations!" Jaycee joyously shouted. First she hugged her friend, then leaned across to hug Scotty.

"She nearly blew it," Scotty said, winking at his fiancée.

Playfully Ruth punched his arm. "You couldn't resist me. I knew it all along."

"If you had continued with your game, I'd have badgered Jaycee into wearing it," he teased.

Jaycee raised her hands to stop the discussion. "Not me. I was miserable." Chuckling, she added, "It looks as though the teacher may have learned a lesson."

All four laughed at the irony. Jonathan's hand beneath the table rested lightly on Jaycee's knee. He seemed as happy about the news as the others.

"You won't believe what he said when he gave it to me," Ruth joined in, laughing. She dismissed the quelling look from Scotty. "He told me I would have to make the last payment on it . . . when I pay the overdue bill for having him file my return last year."

Laughing on the outside, subconsciously Jaycee flinched. The hand on her knee moved up and squeezed. Would the same hands inflaming her senses be the ones padlocking the door on her shop? Could she separate the agent from the man? Compartmentalize her emotions? Her spine stiffened.

"Don't worry," Jonathan whispered, sensing the withdrawal. "You have nothing to fear if everything has been paid. That's a promise."

Everything had been paid, she thought. Louise was efficient about her work. Everything would be fine.

"Come dance with me?"

Jaycee followed Jonathan into the space set aside for dancing. Stepping into his arms was as natural as unlocking the door to her own home. It was the best place she could possibly be.

Swaying to the music, barely moving their feet, they danced in unison. Closing her eyes, Jaycee relished the shoulder-to-knee touching. Fingers locked behind his nape, boldly her thumbs massaged muscles above his shoulders.

"Temptress," Jonathan whispered. Warm breath fanned gently across her face.

"Mmm," she responded as his hands slid up, then back to her hips.

"You're like a cuddly kitten when I touch your back. Stretching, purring, asking for more."

"Turns me on," she confessed softly.

Jonathan chuckled and began stroking her back in earnest.

"Always tell me what you like. I want to please you," he murmured huskily.

"Only if you do the same."

"Woman, just seeing you, watching the copper

87

flecks flash at me, makes me want to . . . well, to use your words—turns me on."

Snuggling closer, she kissed the pulse throbbing on his throat. Smelling the woodsy cologne, she let her tongue flick the vein. Salty, with a tinge of something else, she mused. Trying to decipher the taste, she opened her lips, gently sipping his flavor. Whatever it was, she knew it could become addictive. Before she'd finished tasting, Jonathan made a low guttural sound. Her lips felt the vibration. Gently she nipped his throat.

Immediately his hands clamped against her hips, showing his response. "I'd tell you to stop, but it's too late."

"You taste good," Jaycee said near his ear. Unlacing her fingers, she opened her eyes. One finger circled his ear. Between thumb and forefinger she tested the thickness of his lobe. Dark eyes gazed over his chiseled features.

She remembered thinking how handsome he was when she had first looked up from her desk. Tips of fingers touched the streaks in his sunbleached hair. It was soft. Unbelievably soft and fine. The finger softly raked the side of his face. She wanted to know all the textures of his skin.

Gently Jonathan held her narrow hips while he withdrew. Worried that she'd been too bold, too wanton, she allowed the space to grow. Ducking her head to hide the flush on her cheeks, she barely heard his words.

"The music is about to stop and I need time to . . relax before we go back to the table," he explained softly. "I want you to touch me, but I'm having a heck of a time not reciprocating."

Raising her head, she saw a longing, a hungry expression, before a wide grin flashed, accompanied by a slow wink. One brief, hard kiss later, Jonathan led Jaycee back to the small table.

A split of champagne chilling in a bucket sat in the center of the table with a note propped next to it. Jaycee read it aloud to Jonathan, "Have fun. We decided to drive to Springfield to make the big announcement to Ruth's folks. I paid the tab."

"He paid the tab by signing my name," Jaycee scoffed.

A surprised look made Jonathan's eyebrow cock upward.

"He adds it to my yearly tax bill so it's a deduction for the business. Champagne instead of two martinis." The explanation slipped out before Jaycee remembered she was talking to an IRS agent. "Oooops." Her hand covered her mouth.

"CPA expenses and entertaining a customer are legal deductions," Jonathan stated, smiling at her attempt to keep her tax dodge a secret.

Nervously she lowered her hand. She'd have to watch her mouth. She didn't know enough about tax law to fill a cap for half-inch copper. The wrong slip could land her in a world of trouble.

"You don't, you know," he said quietly.

"Don't what?"

"Have to worry about my gathering information to use against you." Raising her hand, he kissed the soft skin on her inner wrist. "Tuesday I'll request to be taken off your case."

Quietly they drank the bubbly champagne. Both were lost in thought. Jaycee twirled the stemmed glass between thumb and forefinger. If Jonathan were removed from her case, would it make any difference? A locked shop was a locked shop. Her sympathies lay with the small businessman, his with the government. *And never the twain shall meet,* she thought grimly.

Perhaps their thinking had run parallel like the hot and cold water pipes in a house. Each serving a purpose, but never touching.

"Let's go," Jonathan said, standing. His lips were pressed together in a fine line.

Scooting the folding chair back against the wooden planks, Jaycee arose from the table, bumping the flimsy chair against the arm of a man at the next table. "Sorry," she apologized, not looking at the man. Too much introspection was making her clumsy. Jonathan courteously took her elbow, steering her out of the crowd of jubilant holiday vacationers toward the four-story parking garage.

"Want to go skiing tomorrow?" Jonathan asked.

"Want to go fishing?" she answered, demonstrating to herself their professional and recreational differences.

"I'm not much of a fisherman," he replied, warily glancing at Jaycee.

"I'm not much of a skier." Jaycee shook her head at their incapatibility.

"How about meeting at the pool early in the morning?" Jonathan suggested, trying to find a compromise.

"I swim in the lake," she said bluntly in a monotone.

"Are you spoiling for a fight or just being assertive?" Having entered the garage, Jonathan unlocked the passenger door while asking the question. Jaycee climbed into the compact American car, not answering. She could hear his footsteps going around the back of the car. Being unreasonable, unwilling to negotiate, was ridiculous. She silently berated herself. What was she trying to accomplish? Sighing, she knew. Any excuse for incompatibility was easier to find than accepting the possiblity of being emotionally involved.

Jonathan eased behind the steering column. Inserting the key, twisting his wrist, nothing happened. After checking to see that the car was in park, he tried again. Nothing.

"Great!" he muttered. "We'll have to take the van over to your place."

"Your battery terminals are probably corroded. Why don't you clean them rather than leave your car here?"

Reaching down, he released the hood and slowly sat back. "I suppose you know how," he said resignedly.

"Of course. Everybody knows . . ." The disparaging reply caught in her throat behind a giggle. "You don't know how?"

"I play the piano," he said with humor in his voice.

"The piano? Does that help you fix a car?" she asked, puzzled by his statement.

"No. But it explains what I was doing while the boys were out working on their cars." His eyes twinkled with laughter. Leaning to the right, he brushed his lips across hers. "Want to teach me how?"

"If you'll teach me how to ski."

"And you can teach me how to fish."

"And we'll swim . . ." She really did prefer nature's lake water.

"Naked in the lake." His words were uttered before she could compromise further. Their laughter mixed and mingled in the small interior of the car.

Jaycee wrapped her arms around his neck and planted a joyous kiss on his lips. Her spine popped when he crushed her against his chest. His hands moving up, he clasped her head, holding the halo of thick braids. With their lips bonded together their differences were infinitesimal. The here and now was all either of them wanted.

Pulling her head back, she saw him searching for fear, finding only a passionate glow. The hunger she felt was unappeased by one kiss. Dragging his lips back, Jaycee ran her hand beneath his collar to the mat of crisp hair on his chest. Groaning, he lifted her over to his lap.

Twice he tried to break away, pressing his head against her cheek, then he hungrily feasted again. With a tremor running through his hands, he took her shoulders firmly and moved her back to the passenger seat.

"Not in a car like teenagers," he said, swinging his

head from left to right. "I am determined *not* to make love to you in anything less than the comfort of a large bed, but I want you so badly I have the shakes." Proving his point, he stuck his hand out level with the dashboard. The hand trembled slightly.

The vow she heard didn't keep Jaycee's heart from sinking to her stomach. Whatever the choices—love, lust, want, need, temporary, permanent—she knew their desire was mutual.

"Damn!" Jonathan's fist struck the dashboard in frustration. "We both have a house full of guests and the hotel is booked." Futilely he disposed of their options. Closing his eyes, his head dropped back on the headrest.

Jaycee would have smoothed the lines running parallel on his brow, but didn't. Touching him would be like putting a match to a leaky gas tank. The thin line of control over his desire was stretched to the breaking point. Opening the door, she said quietly, "I'll fix the car."

On trembling legs, barely able to support her slight weight, she walked around to the front of the car. Releasing the latch, she opened the hood. She was right. The battery terminals were corroded.

"Any tools in the trunk?" she asked, her voice expanding in the vacuum of the garage.

"None."

Necessity being the mother of invention, she extracted a hairpin anchoring her braids. Scraping the battery post, removing accumulated grime, she fervently hoped the temporary measure would be enough to start the car. Checking the connection leading into the alternator, she said, "Try it."

Hearing the clicking of the starter, she wiggled the cable. Blue sparks flew as the car started. Slamming the hood in her customary fashion, she wiped her hand on the back of her culottes, leaving a dark stain.

Realizing she had just ruined another good outfit, she shook her head in disgust. "Do you have something in here for me to sit on?" Marring the upholstery with grease was the last thing she wanted to do.

Flashing her a smile, Jonathan patted his lap. Chuckling, she shook her head, wrenching her split skirt around, displaying the black handprint. Seeing her predicament, he reached into the back seat, jerking a beach towel forward.

Shortly they were out of the garage headed down the curving road leading to her house. Light flashed into the interior periodically from the streetlamps outside the car.

"Will you take me fishing in the morning?"

"Seven too early?"

"Nothing is too early. I won't sleep tonight."

Jaycee wouldn't sleep either. The night would be spent reliving what had happened . . . and anticipating what would happen.

CHAPTER SIX

"I am going to use worms," Jonathan said emphatically.

They sat at opposite ends of the bass boat in the pedestal armchairs. Dressed in old cut-offs and a tank top, Jaycee felt grubby compared to the red shorts-and-shirt ensemble Jonathan wore.

The previous evening had ended with a chaste kiss at the door, and as predicted, a sleepless night. She was tired . . . and frustrated . . . and irritable with herself for not enjoying her second love, fishing.

"You'll catch only trash fish or blue gill if you use them. I can't teach you to fish if you stubbornly refuse to learn." Irritability made tact impossible.

Slamming his rod into the holder, Jonathan glared at her. "What is wrong with you this morning? You have sniped and snarled since we dropped anchor." Stripping off his shirt, he stood, hands on hips, waiting for an answer.

Jaycee stared mutely at his statuelike physique. Shrugging her shoulders, she twitched the end of the rod. Jonathan dove off the front of the boat into the deep water edging the Palisades. Surfacing, he swam with strong, sure strokes away from the boat.

Twitching the jig, she shut her eyes, closing out Jonathan and the magnificent bluffs soaring steeply a hundred feet into the air.

The mute reply she'd given Jonathan didn't answer his question or her own. Why was she acting like a shrew? Worse than a shrew, she acknowledged to herself. *Bitchy* was the only adequate word describing her actions. Jaycee smiled. *Horny* was the second one. The whole morning was being spoiled by a horny bitch. The self-portrait was ugly.

Reeling in her line, she decided to do something about it. Dropping her rod into the back holder, she stripped to her bathing suit. Seconds later she was in the lake swimming vigorously toward Jonathan.

"Wait up," she yelled. Free style, she closed the distance between them. Jonathan waited, treading water. Less than a stroke away, she lunged for his neck. The kiss she gave him was brutal and swift, plunging them below water. Lips clung, sharing oxygen. The full length of her body was wound around him. Drifting to the surface, the melting together ended as they both gasped for air. Treading water with powerful legs, Jonathan kept them afloat.

Tossing his head back, he roared with laughter. "Thank God! I needed that desperately."

"You could have kissed me," she stated quarrelsomely.

"And have you bite my lip off? No, thanks."

"You were angry when you dove into the lake, but that didn't stop me," she pointed out.

"Next time I'll use your tactic," he replied, grinning. "I was trying to be considerate."

"Well, don't be." Provocatively she wound her legs around his waist. Tracing his lower lip with her tongue, licking off the drops of water, she stopped the smile.

"Let's get out of the main channel if you're going to seduce me." Eyes smoldering, solder color deepening, he raked short-clipped nails down her bare back. "We're going to drown," he cautioned. "I can't keep us afloat in sixty feet of water and make love at the same time." Fingers dug into the back of her rib cage as he pried her away.

"Don't you want to fish," she teased, swirling away and using the crawl to go back to the boat.

Matching her stroke and mood, he answered, "You're too grumpy to fish."

"How about water-skiing then?" she bantered.

Nearing the boat, he grabbed the anchor rope. Arm extended, his free hand circled her wrist. The water between them parted. A strong, muscular arm snaked around her waist, drawing them together.

"How about a physically demanding *indoor* exercise?" he asked pressing their hips together.

"Ping-Pong? Billiards?"

"Mattress polo. It's a new creative game.'

"New? Creative?"

"There are no rules. You make them up as you go along." Strong teeth nibbled her earlobe, sucking the golden post earring between his lips. The teasing note left his voice as it became husky. "I want you badly.

97

You wrapped your legs around me and all I could think of was having you in bed wrapped around me."

A flush spread slowly up from neck to cheeks. Had she been that brazen? Changing from coldly rejecting men's advances to wantonly inviting lovemaking was —her mind groped for the word describing the change—extraordinary.

"It's wonderful. Astounding," she said softly. She didn't realize she'd spoken the words aloud.

"What's wonderful?" Jonathan asked. "My wanting you?"

"No. My wanting you." The warm silky water swirled when she swam toward the short ladder. "Mattress polo it is," she called over her shoulder beguilingly.

By the time she was ready to start the engine, Jonathan had stored the rods and lifted the front anchor. Roaring, the engine came to life. Glancing at Jonathan, she saw him watching the loose tendrils of drying hair being whipped across her face. With nimble dexterity he unclasped the barrette holding her ponytail in place. Satisfaction gleamed from his eyes as he watched it being whipped behind her, blowing freely in the breeze.

The wheel jerked in her hands when he forcefully guided the boat back into the main channel headed in the opposite direction.

Pulling the throttle back, she shouted, "What are you doing?"

"Watching your hair dry. I'll show you where to go." Reaching below her arms, he pushed the throttle back down to full speed.

The front of the boat bucked against the wakes from other, larger boats. Friendly vacationers waved gaily at the speeding bass boat. Returning the waves, Jonathan grinned broadly. He was enjoying the spine-jarring ride. Getting Jaycee's attention by tapping on her shoulder, he motioned for her to turn into the next cove on the right. Shrugging her shoulders, she slowed the boat, gently swerving it into the cove.

"Pull into the second private dock," he instructed her.

"What for? You aren't planning on visiting someone *now* are you?"

"Why not? You don't want to fish or ski?" he teased innocently.

"I sure as hell don't want to go visiting either," she said, turning away from the dock. She couldn't keep the disappointment off her face.

"For once in your hard-headed, independent life, do what you're told to do." The broad grin took the sting out of the order.

Turning sharply, the boat made a U-turn, then slid into the empty dock. Jaycee switched off the engine.

"Who lives here?" Dark eyes swept up the tree-covered hill. A small chalet was tucked into the deep green foliage.

"You'll see," he answered mysteriously.

"I'm hardly dressed to impress anyone," she pointed out, standing, easing the elastic at the bottom of her bright yellow swimsuit.

Agilely Jonanthan jumped to the dock and secured the boat. "You look great—maybe a little overdressed," he continued to tease, raking his eyes down her well-rounded figure.

"This is your aunt's house?" she guessed.

"Nope. Aunt Jess and Kay were only visiting."

"It's your house?"

"Very astute, Ms. Warner," he mocked, giving her a hand out of the boat. "I have a Sun-and-Fun membership at Tan-Tar-A, but I seldom use it. Otherwise I would probably have met you long ago."

Climbing the steep steps, she paused to catch her breath and gather her wits. "Your boat is gone."

"Kay and my aunt are using it to visit relatives at Ha-Ha-Tonka."

"That's thirty miles up the lake. It takes forever to get there and back."

"Visit included, about six to eight hours. But they're spending the night."

Jaycee felt a grin split her lips. What started as a chuckle became a full-blown guffaw. Linking their hands, Jonathan tugged her up the redwood steps leading onto the balcony. The musical laughter was infectious. Without knowing the source of her humor, he joined in.

"I practically kicked Tom out of my house trying to empty it for tonight," she explained, gasping for breath.

"And I told my relatives Uncle George would die from disappointment if they were at the lake and didn't visit him."

"Your place today, my place tonight?" she invited him, slipping her arms around his waist.

"What? No fishing or skiing?" he gently teased, folding her close.

"You're right. It would be a waste to spend this glorious day indoors," she replied spreading her arms wide.

Jonathan swatted her rear end. His hand stayed on her lower cheek to rub the pain away. " 'Come into my parlor,' " he husked.

" 'Said the spider to the fly,' " she said, finishing the line.

"I'm going to devour you from head to toe and back again," he said, lifting her into his arms with ease.

"Expect equal treatment." Clinging to his neck, she began the feast.

Eyes closed, she didn't appreciate the coziness of the living room, or notice the small flight of steps leading upstairs. Her senses were completely involved in absorbing the taste of the salt lake water and a hint of the mysterious flavor always scenting Jonathan's skin.

Gently placed on her feet, gazing into the burning gray eyes, she sensed hesitation in Jonathan. Loosely held, his fingers moved against the bareness of her back.

"Too fast?" he inquired, giving her a chance to change her mind.

Deciding to prolong the anticipation as he had done with his teasing, she turned toward the door. She overheard the groan and the sound of Jonathan sinking into the bed. Quietly she closed the door and shed her swimsuit. Jonathan sat on the side of the bed, hands clasping the back of his neck.

"Too slow," she said softly, walking toward him.

Head jerking up, he stared, unable to mask, not wanting to mask, the desire flaming in his eyes. Full firm breasts swayed with each step. She stepped between his muscular legs. Their eyes locked. Small fingers splayed over deeply tanned shoulders. Drawing him to her, she granted permission to discover the treasure others tried to defile.

"You're more beautiful than I imagined even in my wildest fantasy," she heard in muffled tones.

Leaning back, he brought her down beside him on the bed. Impatient for his caresses, she stroked him from collarbone to waist, over the short shiny hairs, to his flat male nipple. Lips tasted the small bud. It became erect. Chills swept through her. She could hear his heart accelerating under her ministrations.

Long fingers circled sensitive skin, shielding her shoulder blades, spine, and hips. Welded together, hip to hip, chest to chest, Jonathan filled her mouth with the sweet thrusts of his velvet tongue. Breasts hardened, dusky-rose nipples puckered as she arched closer. Taking his hand, she placed it on one mound. His hand opened and closed simultaneously with the thrust in her mouth. A scream of sensuous delight died in the back of her throat, coming out as a groan.

Breaking away, burning eyes never leaving her face, he quickly took off his trunks. Legs straddling, leaning on his elbows, he kissed the tip of each breast. Hands cuddled their fullness together while he alternated attention from one tip to the other.

A fire spread from the erect peaks down to the ache below her stomach. Narrow hips arched in joy, nestling his manhood into dark blond curls at the juncture of her thighs. Jonathan, the musician, was setting the tempo. Slower than a melancholic ballad he stroked and caressed.

"You are so delectably soft," he cooed. "You smell of flowers, and sunshine, and a woman's fragrance all your own."

"Now, Jonathan?" she begged. "Please?"

Ignoring her plea, she felt the roughness of his cheek lower to her navel. Stomach muscles contracted as his warm breath blew over it. Writhing beneath him, she struggled to reach below his waist.

Shaking his head, he said, "I want to know all of you. Every beautiful inch."

An unhurried trail, fiery and moist, went from hip to toe. Hands, lips, tongue, teeth—feeding the volatile fire below the golden skin they touched. Supple hands held her ankles while Jonathan massaged and tongued each toe individually. The soles, terribly ticklish normally, were licked and nipped.

Smiling at the intensely pleasurable sensation, she levered herself higher onto the pillows. Watching the blond head totally absorbed in pleasing her was marvelously sensuous.

His lovemaking was slower than the hour hand on a clock. Nothing was hurried. Time was an unlimited factor. Jaycee realized the extent of his patience, his desire to make their first loving one she'd remember.

As his lips traversed from ankle to the flesh on her inner knees, she also knew he cared deeply. This was not the quick coupling inspired by lust. This was more. The trite expression, "worshipping at the altar of her body," was being brought to life. Each kiss, each stroke, was paying homage to her. Expressing his caring. His love.

Blood rushed to her head. Small screams stuck deep in her chest. The sensations were pleasurable to the point of bordering on pain. How could he control himself when she was falling apart, piece by piece, under his touch. Spiraling upward, she was afraid of reaching the highest peak without him. Frenzied by this fear, she tugged at his head.

Hovering over her, Jaycee willed him into her arching, supplicant body. Lethargically, inch by inch, his manhood sank to the core of her womanhood. Deep, deep within, still he probed farther. Dark eyes flew open, spreading wide.

"Relax, love. Your heat is consuming me." Clutching her hips, he thrust himself to the hilt. Torn apart, she thought. But there was no pain. She had been created to accommodate her love.

Moving together, the frenzy he had built was driving her to an ecstasy utterably unbelievable. Gentle thrusts became hard. They spiraled together. The sun was close. The heat, burning, scorching, they stiffened, reaching the ultimate peak of sexuality. Each cried the other's name in unison.

Short erratic pants brought air into their lungs for their return to the comfortable bed that had been the launching pad for their flight. Raising her shoulders, Jonathan gently moved her trapped hair over one shoulder, then lay beside her.

"It's beautiful," he murmured, threading the honeyed strands through his fingers. Spreading them over himself, he added, "A blanket softer than silk."

Jaycee was tongue-tied. She wanted to express all the emotions she felt, but couldn't. How could she verbalize the elation? The feeling of being one with him? Did he realize the fears he had expelled? *I love him,* she silently mused. Through dark expressive eyes, she communicated her love silently.

"Mine," he said softly against her forehead. The single word branded her brow, reaching her heart.

"Jonathan?"

"Hmm?"

"Thank you."

"Thanks aren't necessary. The gift you gave was exquisite. More precious than anything ever received." The tender expression she saw added depth to his words.

Brushing his lips, she savored their sweetness. Cupping his face as he held hers, she tried to communicate her happiness. She snuggled into the hollow beneath his shoulder. Fighting the heaviness of her lids was a losing battle. She thought she heard Jonathan say "You're mine, Jaycee, love," but it could have been part of her dream.

Jaycee awakened. The tickling sensation traveling over one breast tightening the dusty-rose bud. Contented, she smiled, then stretched.

"You are very sexy when you stretch like that," Jonathan said, smiling down at her. The moistness of his mouth covered the swelling nipple. Stretching again, his teeth grazed the sensitized point.

Drawing up one leg, the outer thigh rubbed against his hardness. "You always up early?" she asked, enjoying the double meaning. Caressing the top of his head with with her fingers and lips, she inhaled deeply when she heard his reply.

"I've been up for quite a while."

Chuckling, she asked, "Do you always wake up" —her hand wrapped around him—"like this?"

Nuzzling both breasts, he groaned her name. Long fingers slipped below her waist, teasing her flesh as she stroked him.

"I let you sleep until I couldn't bear it any longer," he said in the shadowed valley where his head rested. "Are you too tender?" he asked, putting her welfare over his need.

"What would you do if I said yes?"

The hand causing the heat to flow through her veins ceased its erotic movement.

"I may growl like an animal, but I'm not. I would never purposely hurt you."

Rotatating her hips against the palm of his hand made the fingers resume their erotic activity.

"You're driving me wild. Once again, woman, before I totally lose control, are you sore?"

"Mmm. Maybe," she teased, loving the power of controlling this strong, virile man.

"Ah-ha! A tease." The leer she saw and the mischief in his bright gray eyes should have warned her. Rolling swiftly away, he got out of bed and strode to the closet door.

"Jonathan, come back to bed," she coaxed, opening her arms. The enticing picture she made, bare to the waist, honey-blond hair flowing over her shoulders down her back, lips still swollen from their earlier passion, was more temptation than Jonathan could stand.

They fused together instantly. The light-hearted teasing lit a fire Jonathan couldn't control. Roughly he dominated her with his body as she had with words. Their lovemaking was swift, complete, bordering on savage.

When their breathing quieted, Jonathan said huskily, "Did I hurt you? I've never lost myself in lovemaking like that. You're too sexy for your own good."

"No, you didn't hurt me. But, in all honesty, we'd better not spend the whole day in bed or I won't be *able* to leave."

The tenderness she had seen earlier was still in his eyes. The same caring tenderness could be heard in his voice.

"I love you, Jaycee Warner."

"I'm in love with you too, Jonathan Wynthrop," she whispered.

Kissing her uptilted nose, her lover chuckled. "I was beginning to wonder if you'd tell me. Say it again, louder."

"I love you. I love you. I love you." Each word became louder in volume.

Laughing in the joy of discovering love, they clung to each other.

"How about a quick shower and lunch?" he asked, squeezing her soft, round behind.

Getting out of bed, they crossed the rust-colored

carpeting leading into the bathroom. Navy blue towels accented the pure white fixtures. Wallpaper blended navy, rust, and gold in thin stripes. It was masculine. As pure in line and as well balanced as the man who owned it.

Jaycee stood before the full-length mirror on the back of the door as Jonathan turned the shower faucets on. *I don't look any different,* she thought, somewhat surprised. Touching the puffiness of her lower lip, she amended the first appraisal. There was a fresh glow to the tone of her skin that hadn't been there before. A faint rim of copper color edged the dark irises of her eyes. Love and being loved had transformed her from an attractive girl into a radiant woman.

Jonathan silently moved behind her. The mirror framed their images as if for a formal picture. His wet hands stole around her waist.

"Admiring my woman?" he asked lightly.

"Checking for damage."

"No bruises, I hope." Swiftly his eyes raked over her shoulders, back, and hips. Damp hands rose, cupping the fullness of both breasts. Chin sweeping her hair back, he kissed the nape of her neck.

Watching their combined reflection made Jaycee think of a bedroom with walls and ceiling completely covered with mirrors. Being able to watch both their movements was strangely exciting. *Kinky,* she thought, trying to admonish herself for extending the erotic blend of images dancing before open eyes.

"You're like a fine wine. Full-bodied, deliciously flavored, tempting to the palate." His velvet tongue tasted her skin. One hand slid to her waist. One finger circled her navel, dipping in and out. "I'll never be able to have enough of you."

Leaning back against him, silky hair the only curtain between them, Jaycee closed her eyes. Steam adhering to the coolness of the glass distorted her view. The magic of his hands and words combined with the mirrored image was too overwhelming.

"Back to bed?" she suggested.

"No," he whispered, denying the desire they both felt. Releasing, then turning her pliant body to face him, he promised, "Later." Lips barely touching, he sealed the promise before heading toward the shower, taking her along.

The water, first warm then cold, was invigorating. Efficiently he lathered her from head to toe, but didn't linger. The disappointment she felt was tempered when Jonathan explained with a wink that mattress polo was exhausting and players needed recovery time between bouts to heal and regain their strength and stamina.

After coating him with Ivory lather she said with admiration, "You have a great body for a tax agent."

"For a plumber, you have the best in town," he retorted, smiling broadly.

"Was that a compliment?" she asked. She was the *only* woman plumber in town. Splashing the soapy washcloth over his chest, she scoured him like a dirty copper fitting.

"My exact thought before I returned the compliment." Jonathan moved under the pelting water, flushing the clinging suds from his skin.

It had been a back-handed compliment, she silently agreed. *How do you tell a man he has the body of a Greek god without it sounding silly. All the phrases I think of are like something out of a badly written film. The plumbers' code book didn't prepare me for anything like this!* Jaycee promised herself to start listening for lyrics to songs and reading romantic books. It pained her to be such a novice at the art of expressing her love. For now the best she could do was . . .

Backing him out from under the downpour into the corner of the small enclosure, she said, "I'm still a Missourian. I'll *show* you a flesh and blood compliment."

"Oh, no, you won't. Not until later, my love." Cocking a wet eyebrow, he countered, "First we eat. Second we spend several hours frolicking. Third . . . we'll see how proud of your home state you are."

Jaycee's laughter at the proposed agenda acknowledged her acceptance. Scrupulously followed, it would have him panting at her feet before the sun sank into the west.

110

CHAPTER SEVEN

The question had bothered her all morning. She wanted to ask, but the aura of happiness could burst with an untimely remark. Something was out of place. It was as though she were in a building and didn't know when to reduce the three-inch copper to two-inch, or had forgotten whether the hot water main was at the front of the center joist or the back.

"Get it off your chest before you chew up the inside of your cheek," Jonathan said with perception. "You'll catch more if the tip of your rod isn't in the water."

"The tip isn't in the water. I'm letting the jig sink to the bottom," she retorted indignantly. The missing piece to the puzzle had kept her from watching her line, but she couldn't admit that to a novice. She'd been known to fish the bottom. *Yeah,* she thought, *when I'm figuring out a particularly rocky business problem. Since he knows something is bothering me, I might as well be forthright and ask.*

"Jonathan? How can a government employee afford a house on the lake and a high-powered ski boat?"

"Bribes."

The rod nearly fell from her hands into the thirty feet of water below the boat. "Bribes?" she squeaked in a disbelieving, high-pitched voice. Jaycee stared in shock at Jonathan, who leisurely continued to dip his jig rather than twitch the tip.

"Sure," he replied. "That's why I followed you to the lake and had Kay deposit me within yards of your boat. The hook in my leg wasn't planned . . . that *was* an accident. The rest was easy. Get your confidence. Have a quick romp in the hay. Tell you how much I need to take care of your problem, and how I can provide 'special services.' You're well off. You told me so yourself. I'll even take a company check. Write it off your taxes for next year." A closed mask kept any expression from his face. The explanation was given in the same grim voice he'd used when informing her about the court order and padlock. The rod had stopped dipping, His hands gripped the butt tightly, knuckles white.

Confused, she couldn't immediately tell whether he was telling the truth or stringing together a pack of lies. What he'd said didn't jibe with what she intuitively knew about the man. Had she been wrong? Was he guilty of what he'd confessed to? The newspapers were full of stories about bribery and corruption. Government officials, union officials, senators, representatives, were indicted when caught and often found guilty. Had the IRS agent led her up the garden path to get into the bank vault?

Jaycee vehemently shook her head from left to right. "I don't believe that story. Try another."

112

A rakish smile split his handsome face. The rod began arcing back and forth.

"You suspected the worst. I decided to confirm your suspicions." The wink she had grown to love flashed. "What's the matter, Jaycee, afraid I'm going to live off your wealth?" he teased.

"Fat chance. *No* man is going to use me!"

"My sentiments exactly . . . only vice versa."

"You mean you think I gave sexual favors so you'd use your influence to get me out of the jam with the IRS?" Her temper was beginning to flare.

"Is that worse than your thinking I seduced you for money?" A deep red stain was creeping up his neck under the golden tan.

Voice lowering as she fought to control her temper, she said, "Well! How the hell do you afford those luxuries?" The tip of her rod splashed into the lake's surface.

"I'm an attorney studying tax law, working with the IRS. And quit cursing around me!" he bellowed.

Mouth gaping, she stared at Jonathan. How many times had she told him he couldn't afford her? The man had a law degree. He was probably rich. Closing her mouth, she shook her head, as if shaking it would help her digest the information he'd shouted at her. He was smart, rich, and handsome. Women probably fell all over him, she thought bleakly. Sophisticated, beautiful debutantes, the cream of St. Louis society, were the sort of women he was used to. This wasn't going to work.

Jonathan gripped her upper arms. "Now, what's

going through that crazy blond head of yours?" he demanded, his voice still slightly raised.

"Nothing," she muttered, not looking at him.

Roping her ponytail around his wrist, he jerked down, raising her head. Jaycee closed her eyes, not wanting him to see the doubts plaguing her.

"Open your eyes!" he commanded, tugging again.

Clenching her teeth against the sharp pain at the back of her head, she refused, squeezing her eyes tightly shut.

"I can't tell what you are thinking if you don't open your eyes." He tugged a second time.

"If you pull my hair again, I'm going to knock your butt right out of this boat," she threatened, meaning every word.

Jonathan chuckled. Slowly, deliberately, he began kissing her, while stroking her back and pulling her off the chair into his embrace.

Squirming, she tried to gain release. Stubbornly she kept her eyes closed. "Let go of me," she muttered against his lips.

"No."

The harder she pushed, the tighter the steel bands held her. It was like one of those Chinese wicker puzzles she stuck her fingers in as a child. The harder she would pull, the tighter the wicker bit into the fingers. The only way to solve the puzzle was to relax. Now she did.

The warm, sensuous male lips began demanding a response. Force she could repel, and often had, but gentle persuasion was invincible. Slender arms stole around his neck.

114

"Kiss me, Jaycee," he coaxed, spreading minute kisses on the corners of her lips. One knee nudged between her tender thighs as her lips spread apart.

Denial was impossible. Groaning, she pulled the probing thrusts in deeper. Convulsively, using all her strength, she held him. All logic was pushed aside by the desire to be part of him.

A horn hooting ended what had only begun. "Give her one for me," she heard over the roar of the speeding boat.

Jonathan held her close. A drop of perspiration slid down her cheek. The fleshy tip of his fingers wiped it away.

"Love, love, what am I going to do with you," he murmured. "You infuriate and excite me more than I care to tell you."

"That boat is turning around," she mumbled against his neck. "Want to give them something to write home about?"

"What we have I don't want to share with any-one," he growled, stepping away, turning toward the front deck.

Watching him walk away was a visual delight. A well-muscled back tapered to a narrow waist. As he bent to retrieve his rod, his buttocks flexed. Dark swim trunks stretched over the hard, taut muscle. The hair immediately below them was darker, coars-er, than the platinum hairs covering the rest of his muscular legs. *Nice,* she thought. *Very nice.*

Articles had been written in magazines about male fetishes: legs, breasts, long hair. Editors were missing a good opportunity. Her eyes swept over Jonathan's shoulders, waist, rear, and legs. Which would her fetish be? When he turned, she watched the muscles on his chest ripple as he put his hands on his hips. Tilting her head up, she saw his eyes gleaming brightly. The decision was easy. A smile hovered on her lips. *An eyes woman,* she thought. *That's what attracted me first.*

"Enjoying yourself?" Jonathan asked, the gleam acknowledging her careful appraisal.

"You have a great body, even from the back," she said simply, honestly, not trying to evade the question.

Jonathan laughed self-conciously. "You don't mince words, do you?"

"Do you want me to?"

"Absolutely not. Your candidness is refreshing. One of your most appealing traits."

Striking a bathing-queen pose, she asked, "Are you sure?"

"On second thought," he chuckled, "it's your mechanical genius I appreciate the most." He teased her, seemingly ignoring the large, firm breasts thrusting upward over a trim waist and shapely, slender legs.

Swaying her hips seductively, she walked toward him, stopping within touching distance. Languidly reaching up, she released the clasp, allowing her hair to spill down her back. Nimble fingers parted the hair in back, pulling the long tresses over her breasts. One arched eyebrow lifted.

Clapping his hands, he asked, "Are you trying to get ravished in the bottom of the boat?"

116

A cheeky grin replaced the sultry smile. "I just wanted to see if my 'mechanical mind' was all that turned you on." Dark eyes slid to the front of his trunks. "You are a liar, Jonathan Wynthrop."

One long index finger followed the fabric at the top of her swimsuit. "And you are asking for more than you can handle. But enough of this unseemly talk, lady. How about we take a ride down to the dam?"

"The damned what?" She couldn't resist twisting his last word.

"The darned dam," he succinctly replied. "Now you don't have a choice." Stepping back on the deck, he began raising the anchor. "You're too old to spank or wash your mouth out with soap. I'll work out a system of forfeits. This time your fishing is forfeited." The anchor clunked into its holder. Agilely he bound over the bench seats to the back anchor.

"Who gave you the right to mete out punishments?" she demanded, refusing to let anyone dictate to her.

"You did."

"The hell you say."

Jonathan's eyes looked up to the sky, but he continued raising the back anchor. "Now I'm not going to buy you any fudge at the candy factory."

"I'll buy my own damned candy," she proclaimed, stressing the curse word.

"No T-shirt either." Towering over her, he gritted out the punishment between rigid jaws. "You're being childish. Keep your mouth rolling and I'll reconsider the method of punishment."

"You'd better never hit me, mister," she spat out.

"I'll have you flat on your back before you make contact."

Tossing his head back the way he always did when he was really amused, he roared with laughter. The deep tones rumbled up from his chest. Never had a man laughed at her when she was angry enough to spit copper fittings.

"Darn you," she yelled, restraining from stomping her foot.

"Love, you can throw me on my back anytime." Creases, laugh lines, crinkled the corners of his eyes. "Believe me, once there, we'll forget about the crime *and* the punishment."

Jaycee's sense of humor surpassed her anger. Before she could clamp her hand over her mouth, musical giggles had bubbled out.

Sliding behind the steering wheel, still chuckling, she said, "I'll watch my mouth!"

Joining her on the seat, he bent forward and picked up the barrette she'd dropped earlier. The golden clasp caught the sun's rays, momentarily blinding him. Jaycee saw him blinking rapidly. It made a plunking noise when he pitched it over the side. Her hand wasn't fast enough to retrieve it.

"Before you strip a yard of hide off me," he said, raising his hands defensively in front of his face, "that was pure reflex. It blinded me for a second and . . . I've always hated the darned thing anyway." Lowering his arms, one hand lifted a long strand of gold as his voice became husky. "I prefer it loose. Blowing wild. Uninhibited." Silver eyes simmered. "Like you."

Kissing the beloved hand, she said with sincerity, "I don't think any man has ever made me feel more desirable or feminine. Thank you."

"You are a constant surprise. One minute you're icy, the next you're blowing fireballs, and then you're completely disarming by thanking me so sweetly." Kissing the hair still clinging to his hand, he muttered, "I love you."

"I love you too," she concurred, softly kissing the top of his sunstreaked hair.

"Start the engine. We're back on dangerous territory," he said as he looked into her dark eyes. "The copper fires are burning brightly."

The roaring engine made conversation impossible. Occasionally Jonathan would wave to a skier or point to a house bordering the lake. Jaycee showed him the houses that were her favorites. They both seemed to prefer the ones with long windows and natural cedar siding.

In one day she had learned so much about him. The fears she'd had magically disappeared with the new knowledge. For the first time she felt loved and cherished. Their sexual compatibility was part of this love, but the meshing and blending of ideas and values were equally important.

Jonathan wasn't going to let her tread all over him, but he didn't push her ideas aside as unimportant or irrelevant. Openly declaring his love first had made him vulnerable. Jaycee treasured the vulnerability. The weapon he'd trusted her with had a potential danger. Jaycee laughed to herself. Jonathan was too strong to die from a broken heart, she thought wryly, but he could be easily hurt if she were to wield the power ruthlessly.

Glancing at him, her smile widened. Relaxed, the wind was whimsically disarranging his hair. The sun deepening his tan was tinging the bronze flesh red. He returned her smile. Strong, white, even rows of teeth shone through his lips. She was damned lucky. *Darned* lucky, she mentally amended. *I'll clean up my language just to please him.*

The afternoon was spent in typical tourist fashion. They ambled through the shops, investigating the nooks and crannies selling tourist novelties. Many of the shops displayed wooden plaques with homespun wisdom. Jonathan particularly enjoyed one that read RELATIVES AND FISH STINK AFTER THREE DAYS.

Passing the candy factory, Jaycee read their slogan aloud: "Best candy by a dam site."

Jonathan grabbed her hand and strode away. Even when she pleaded prettily for a pound of fudge, she was ignored.

"I'll buy my own candy if you'll let go of my hand."

Jonathan strode on in silence.

"Please . . . ?"

"Sorry." Determination was evident in the double syllable.

"My gigantic sweet tooth will perish if it isn't stuffed with dark, creamy, chocolate fudge," she continued.

Stopping in front of a jewelry store he asked, "Would you consider a swap? You quit nagging me about the candy and I'll buy you a T-shirt. Or a piece of jewelry," he bargained, cupping his hands to the side of his face to block the glare from the window.

Teeth sinking into his bare arm, Jaycee agreed, saying, "I've sworn off sweets anyway. Found something more satisfying."

Laughter remedied any hidden hostility. Jonathan bought a T-shirt emblazed with I BELONG TO and a big arrow pointing to the right. He made a great show of keeping on her right side at all times. Jaycee basked in the warmth of his sunny personality. He constantly amused and delighted her with his sharp wit.

Stopping in front of a pizza parlor, they watched fascinated as the chef twirled the pizza dough high into the air. Noticing he had an audience, he threw it higher and higher. When the dough became the correct size, he beckoned them in. They couldn't resist.

The pizza was scrumptious. Thick cheese, oozing, formed long strings from the pizza pan to their mouth. What Jaycee would normally have considered sloppy became sensuous. Jonathan's tongue flicking out, wrapping the cheese around it, and swallowing, reminded her of other, more exquisite uses. As if having received a telepathic message, Jonathan watched her eating.

"Tom Jones should have eaten pizza. Definitely erotic," he commented. Using a napkin, he wiped tomato sauce from the edge of her mouth.

Hours, smiles, laughs, later, they pulled into Jaycee's private dock. Together they fastened the boat down and put away the fishing tackle. Hand in hand they walked into the cool air-conditioned cabin, heading straight for the master bedroom. Sexual tension had been building all day. The glances, the accidental touching, the smiles, were the foreplay to their coming together.

Their lovemaking was as leisurely as the day had been. Each thrilled to the other's touch. Haste would have destroyed the final culminating impact. Loving was like sky diving. Getting in the plane and jumping out before it soared into flight would be wasted effort. The thrill was in the anticipation, then the participation of free falling through open space. Circling, twisting, arching, they soared, held together intimately, as though their lives were dependent upon reaching a common goal. The hushed words of love were as undistinguishable as the shouts of a sky diver.

"I can't believe that each time it's better," Jaycee said, her voice filled with wonder.

"Think what we have to look forward to," Jonathan replied, predicting a glorious future.

"Mmm," she said before stretching and cuddling close to his side. "Better and better."

Silently Jaycee's bare feet ascended the carpeted steps. Serving her lover breakfast in bed was a fantasy she wanted to fulfill. Knowing her own limited capability in the kitchen, she had planned the menu while watching Jonathan sleep.

Careful not to clang the pots and pans around, she filled one with hot water, dropping in two eggs, and turned the burner on under it. Coffee was easy. Within seconds it was dripping, aromatically filling the air. She buttered the bread and popped it into the toaster-oven. The small box of dry cereal she chose had to be the correct one.

"Breakfast of champions," she said, muttering the cereal's slogan. "Couldn't be more apropos."

Mentally she ticked off a list of everything needed: cereal, milk, silverware, napkin, egg cups, salt, pepper.

"Damn, I wish I had a flower," she muttered. Slapping her mouth, she corrected herself, "*Darn.*"

Tray filled, Jaycee padded down the steps back into the bedroom. Jonathan was awake. Dressed only in a broad grin, he was propped up against the pillows.

"Breakfast in bed?" he asked, helping her with the tray.

"Befitting a king," she proclaimed immodestly.

"What more could I ask for? A tray brimming with . . . gourmet delights and a lusty serving-wench."

"Was 'gourmet delight' a slam at my lack of cooking ability?" she asked defensively.

Chuckling, Jonathan replied, "Can we save round one for later? I'm famished." The wink was far too appealing to resist. With a kingly flourish, he snapped the cloth napkin and spread it over his bare lap.

Jaycee joined him on the bed and they quickly consumed the feast. Jonathan admitted to never having eaten breakfast in bed, but thought the idea was great. Amidst eating and quiet laughter, they

123

planned their day. Both skirted all around the imminent departure that evening, but neither of them had the heart to discuss the leavetaking.

Carrying the tray upstairs, Jonathan was unusually silent. Jaycee chattered like a magpie. Inane words kept popping out. *Shut up,* she told herself, then went into a long spiel about Missouri weather. Jonathan watched her flit from counter to sink, hands moving in tempo with her mouth.

"Jaycee . . ." he interrupted just as she was launching into the facts about last year's snowstorm, "what's wrong? You're like a wind-up doll with the mainspring about to snap."

Hand clamped over her mouth, she walked into the living room and collapsed on the couch. Scared, she thought, identifying the cause of her untypical behavior. *Plain old scared.* Shuddering, she clasp her knees to her chest.

The cushion next to her sank down with Jonathan's weight. Gently he drew her against his chest. "You've said a thousand words in the last few minutes. Tell me what is wrong."

"I'm scared sh . . . silly," she said, changing the foul word into an acceptable one.

"Scared? The lady plumber that runs her own business singlehandedly, defies the union by becoming a member, and spits fire and brimstone at the federal government is scared? Of what?" he asked.

"Of losing you," she answered with honest simplicity.

Jonathan raised her head. Cupping her face warmly in his hands, he responded, "*That* is impossible.

124

I'm not the kind of man who gets lost in the shuffle. Come on, Jaycee. We aren't flying off to opposite ends of the globe. We both live in the same city."

"But you might decide this was a holiday fling," she said with depression in her voice.

"I might do a lot of things, but that isn't one of them."

"You probably date those toothpaste-ad society girls," she continued perversely.

"Come on, honey. I'm thirty-four years old. Would you feel better if I told you I dated only women with snakes in their hair?"

The effort he made to add levity to their conversation was lost. Jaycee was slowly sinking farther and farther into her own emotional quagmire.

"I'm practically a high-school dropout. You're too big a fish for a minnow."

Kissing her ear, he murmured something very explicit that made Jaycee laugh half-heartedly. Chuckling, he pulled her onto his lap.

"We have a whole day to reassure each other," he said, raking his day-old beard over her neck.

"Quit it. You'll give me a whisker burn." Secretly she thrilled at the rough stubbles branding her. "I like it," she confessed.

"Stop . . . go . . . quit . . . don't quit. I'm the one that should worry about a change of heart," he playfully said, raking her neck again. "Those macho men inhabiting construction sites are pretty formidable opposition." His lips thinned grimly. He hugged her close.

"*That* is ridiculous. I was raised on job sites. Macho types don't interest me."

"You admired my body," he pointed out. "Don't you look at theirs?" he asked, baiting the trap.

"When I employ a man, I'm not interested in his chest measurements," she scoffed.

"But you have dated them?"

"Casually. I'm particular. I'd rather stay home and read than fight in the front seat of a car."

The trap snapped. "You answered your own doubts. You've been around macho men and I've been around society women. Neither of them suit our particular tastes." Teeth nipping her ear, he emphasized how delectable she was.

Jaycee still had the gut feeling they had come too far too fast and were tempting the gods by flaunting their happiness. Why didn't love come with a guarantee? It was a high risk commodity. There was no point in silently debating the problem; Jaycee knew she would have to take the same risks that every other woman did when she fell in love.

"Want to learn how to ski?" Jonathan asked, beginning to organize the day's activities.

"Can we compromise?"

"How?"

"You ski; I'll tube."

"You've got a deal," he enthused.

"Hold on tight!" Jonathan shouted over the inboard engine of the ski boat.

Jaycee went limp on the huge tractor inner tube. The ski rope twanged, the tube jerked, water surged over her, but she remained relaxed. Moments later the powerful boat was out of the bucket and skimming the top of the water. Jaycee raised her fist, thumb up, signaling to go faster. Feet bouncing, she tried to rudder herself across the wake. Seeing the attempt, Jonathan swung the boat in a wide circle. The tube and its occupant popped over the wake. Jaycee laughed.

She loved tubing. It was nearly impossible to make her fall off. The boat zigzagged. Jonathan was trying to shake her off. Raising her fist, she stuck her thumb up again.

Trees became a blur at the higher speed. He circled again. Limply her body flopped from side to side, but she remained on the tube. Making the circle tighter, she was bucked over wake after wake. A cruiser passed, adding to the turbulent water. Jaycee was tossed in the air, landing flat on her back. Swimming to the surface, she came up laughing.

Bringing the boat around, Jonathan shouted, "Are you okay?"

"Yeah! That's a blast!"

The boat nosed closer. Jonathan cut the engine. "That is the most fantastic ride I have ever seen. I thought I'd run out of gas before you popped off."

Climbing up the back ladder, Jaycee flung herself into the cushioned seat. Merriment danced in her eyes. "Try it."

"No, thanks," he replied fervently, shaking his head. "The tube bounces, beats, then tries to drown me. I'll stick to my ski."

Hand over hand he hauled in the ski rope, dragging in the bulky black tube. Wedging it between the back bench and the front chair, he untied the yellow nylon rope.

"Jonathan, we need a watcher."

"There aren't many boats on the lake. You can drive and watch. Just be careful."

Earlier he had let Jaycee take a practice run to learn how to pull a skier, but Jaycee was nervous about being solely responsible for the boat *and* the skier.

What if she didn't see a submerged log? He could be seriously injured and it would be her fault. A knot began forming in her throat. Hadn't this same boat nearly collided with her bass boat?

"Darn it! It's dangerous!"

He threw the ski and rope over, donned his life vest and jumped overboard. "Now you have to do it. Slide forward slowly until the rope is tight. I'll give the signal. Slam the throttle down. Once we've planed out, hold the speed at thirty-five rpm's."

Jaycee carefully followed his instructions and within minutes Jonathan was out of the water, skiing on one ski. He swerved, zigzagging back and forth over the wake. She kept one eye on what was in front of the boat and the other on Jonathan. Water swished high over his head with each jump. He was beauty in motion.

Sticking one leg straight in front of him, he slowly bent into a squat position, then released the skibar with one hand, raising it high over his head. Seconds later he was back in an upright position, waving at her. His head was tossed back. She knew he was laughing hard. The tricks he performed were complicated. They required timing and balance. Kay was right. Jonathan was one fantastic skier. Finally he tossed the rope and sank into the water, never losing balance.

"Wow!" Jaycee shouted, hugging him as he climbed into the boat.

"To put it in your words, 'That's a blast.' The driver deserves a kiss." Briefly, firmly, he kissed her waiting lips. "Want to go look at my ceiling or your ceiling?" he murmured.

"Mine." The smile on her face reflected her happiness.

Lying in bed, snuggled closely to Jonathan, Jaycee rediscovered the softness of the hair blanketing his chest. The tang of aftershave had been washed away by lake water. Only his own special fragrance was left.

"Mmm. You smell so good," she said, licking his collarbone.

Lazily Jonathan trailed his hand down her back. Fingers twining in her hair, he spread its length over his chest.

"What a beautiful silk blanket," he murmured against her forehead. "Don't ever cut it." With the flat of his palm he rubbed the softness from his chest to waist.

"Is that an order?"

"No. A request," he answered, chuckling. "You'd be at the beauty parlor first thing in the morning if I ordered you to leave it long."

"That is not true," she protested immediately. "I'd leave it long because it's convenient. I can braid it, twist it on top of my head, and it's out of the way when I have to wear a hard hat."

"Very practical," he said, still sensuously rubbing it over himself.

Jaycee stilled his hand and began caressing her hair against him with her own fingers.

"Feels good, little temptress," he groaned, pulling her closer. "I'll miss you tonight."

"Hinting?"

"We could drive back to St. Louis and stay together."

Jaycee considered the offer. Having departed hastily Friday, she knew the work vans needed to be restocked. That meant arriving at the shop long before six o'clock. Being in love didn't alter the demands of running a business.

"You're welcome to come to my house," she offered. "I have to be at the shop early . . . early . . . early."

"Do you have a suit that's not too frilly for me to wear to work?" he teased.

"No, but I have closets filled with men's suits."

Jonathan drew back, piercing her soft brown eyes.

"My dad's," she explained, laughing at the conclusion he'd jumped to.

"Funny, lady," he growled. "Living with your parents would defintely cramp my style."

"Oh! I don't live with them. Dad retired and they're in Phoenix."

"Roommate?" he inquired.

"Just me."

"Not for long . . . I hope."

Jonathan's warm mouth covered hers. Languidly Jaycee stroked his face. As the tip of his tongue probed, asking entrance, she knew he was asking for more. Would she let him move in? He wanted to live with her. Parting her lips, she accepted more than the deepening kiss. She wanted him. Now. Later. Forever.

Passion's fires flamed. His hand trailed over the path from breast to concave waist, over smooth thigh, and back again. As his fingers returned up her back, a small purring noise left her throat, escaping into his mouth. Jonathan lay her flat on her stomach on the flowered sheets. Sitting astride her legs, he began scratching the sensitive skin in rounded circles that began at her shoulder blades, and dropped to the base of her spine.

The purring became a low moan when his fingertips were replaced by the sandpaper texture of his cheeks.

Inhaling deeply, Jaycee buried her face in the pillow. The fragrance of clean bedlinen mixed with the odor of Jonathan's cologne and perspiration was an aphrodisiac. Her fingers clenched the pillow's softness, her hands kneading it as though it were Jonathan's shoulders.

Sharp teeth nipped at the tender flesh, bone by bone down the spine his teeth and tongue flicked. Aching intensely, her hips rose when he touched the center of her nervous system at the spine's base. The natural movement of her hips was arousing Jonathan

131

and, unable to wait a moment longer, he turned her to face him. The tip of his manhood pressed into her waiting warmth and once again they were taking each other higher and higher, whispering words of love that added to their overwhelming pleasure.

Jaycee was neither pupil nor teacher. Jonathan had gently, tenderly, caringly, excited every nerve ending, preparing her for lovemaking. She had done the same. Love, passion, and desire were the teachers, Jonathan and Jaycee, the eager pupils. They pleased each other.

Afterward, satiated, Jonathan soothed the tremors that shook her body. Turning her over on her back, gentle hands pulled dampened tendrils away from her face. Tender lips brushed over her moist forehead.

"You have the most beautiful navel," he whispered, one finger circling the rounded indentation.

Chuckling, Jaycee asked, "Aren't all bellybuttons alike?"

"No way. Some are oval. Some are little slits. Others sort of sag. Your is perfect."

"Good obstetrician. Mother was attracted by his ad in the yellow pages. 'For the perfect navel, call 111–1111.' "

The open stream of conciousness conversation following their loving was the time she loved most. His voice was soft and husky; hers was deep and melodious. They shared trivial information about friends, childhood antics, and occasionally dreams important to each of them. Jonathan became her friend and confidant as well as lover.

"Will I see you tomorrow night?" Jonathan asked, tenderness reflected in his eyes.

"What about tonight? Decide to go home to your own bed?"

"Uh-huh. We don't have to rush. We have all the time in the world." He squeezed Jaycee closer. "I'll miss you though."

"Mmm. I'll miss you too."

"Come over to my house and I'll fix dinner for us."

"Don't trust my cooking ability, huh?" she teased, playfully tweaking the hair below his collarbone.

"You have other, more important attributes," he said, his eyes crinkling with laughter. "I still need the terminals cleaned on my battery."

Waving small fingers before his eyes, then running them down the front of his body, she said, "I'll clean your cables," in a low, threatening voice.

"And recharge my battery?" he asked, laughing huskily.

"Your eyes are luminous at times," she joked.

"So are those copper flecks," he murmured, no longer teasing. Swiftly he kissed both eyelids.

Moving the tangled bedlinen away from their feet, he said, "Time to head back, love."

Jaycee nodded. The sweet bliss was temporarily ended, but tomorrow was another day. All her tomorrows would be filled with Jonathan. The words were synonymous . . . weren't they?

CHAPTER EIGHT

The stale air was hot and sticky. The odor of oil, metal, and glue blended into a heavy mugginess. Jaycee turned on the overhead fan. The slow, whirring blades lifted the smell to the high ceiling of the garage.

Removing the clipboard from each van's dashboard, she did a mental inventory of the supplies used. Being on a job and not having the right fitting or valve was frustrating to the plumber and costly to the company. Carefully Jaycee restocked supplies used the previous work day. Tearing the forms off the pad, she folded them together to use later when reordering from the supply house.

Being organized was the key to running a small business. Jaycee thumped the rear fender of the first van she'd bought and pushed the button opening the garage doors.

"Ready and waiting," she said with pride.

The back door to the office was unlocked. Louise White was inside making coffee. Jaycee's nose twitched, welcoming the fragrance.

"Hi, Louise. How was the short but sweet vacation?"

"Fine, hon." Blue eyes twinkled merrily in her round chubby face. "Having grandkids your age sure makes a person feel old." Imitating the hobbling of the very aged, she moved to her desk.

"You'll never be old," Jaycee said, flashing a warm smile.

"Working for you keeps me too busy to slip into senility," she teased, waving a hand at the account book and suppliers' bills. "Give me the supply replacement lists and I'll tally them up. You must have been busy Friday," she said after glancing over the list.

Easing into her own dilapidated chair, Jaycee leaned back. The creaking noise brought Ruth's head up.

"You'll need to get the tax files out and the checks written to Uncle Sam." Clearing the IRS mess up was foremost on her mind. Now that Louise was back, the problem should be easily resolved.

"Why? Is there a problem?" Louise's eyes dropped away from Jaycee. Nervously she fidgeted with the white forms in her hands.

The old chair seemed to moan in protest as Jaycee stood up. "You tell me. The IRS was here Friday. They were ready to shut the doors." Jaycee watched Louise gulp. A small nerve twitched at the corner of her eye. "We are in the clear, aren't we?"

Silently Louise stood, head down, and walked to the files. At the back of the bottom file drawer she pulled out a thick manila envelope. Wordlessly she placed the file in front of Jaycee's bent elbows.

"What's this?" Jaycee asked, not opening the folder.

"Warning letters."

"But . . . how could this happen? You deposit money into the savings account weekly to pay the taxes." Jaycee was completely baffled. Louise had taken care of the employee taxes for years. What could have gone wrong? Oh, no, she thought, feeling an iciness enter her blood, chilling her marrow. The IRS didn't make a mistake. She *was* a T.D.

The twinkle had fled Louise's eyes, replaced by abject misery. "I borrowed the money."

She heard Louise's words, but they didn't seem to sink in. All she knew was Jonathan Wynthrop would be back . . . with a padlock. The blood drained from her face, leaving it a pasty white.

"Come again?"

"I borrowed the money. I needed it to get my grandson, Bob, out of trouble," she answered flatly. "I sent the forms in to the IRS. I just never sent the money."

"How much did you . . . borrow?"

Jaycee gasped when she heard the amount. "When?"

"Three years ago. I have the money to pay it back, but I didn't know how to do it without telling you." Tears began to fall down the wrinkled face.

"Why didn't you ask for the money you needed? You know I'd have loaned it to you?"

The question was as painful to ask as it would be

136

to answer. Jaycee wasn't angry, but she wanted an explanation. How could a person she totally trusted violate the bond they had built over the years?

"You didn't have the money," Louise answered between sniffles. "Bob was seventeen. He let his insurance lapse and had a car accident. It wiped out my savings for the lawyers and I used your tax money for the settlement."

Jaycee's mind whirled back to her financial status three years back. Buying her father out and making the down payment on the lake house had eliminated her reserve cash and put a strain on her credit. Every penny had been spent on running the business and repaying the loans.

"Louise. Oh, Louise," she groaned miserably. "You should have told me. We'd have worked it out. Dad would have helped."

"He couldn't. The money you paid him was spent on that fancy house in Phoenix." Louise shook her head sorrowfully. "I'm ashamed, Jaycee. You've been good to me and I am such a coward. Bob and I saved up the money, but I had too much pride to tell you. Hiding those letters didn't make them go away." She circled her neck with one hand. Small beads of sweat appeared on her upper lip. "I'm sorry I let you down, hon. You've worked so hard and I . . ." She didn't complete the sentence. Like a withered leaf, she crumpled on the desk.

"Oh, my God. Louise . . ." Jaycee rushed around the desks. "Heart attack." Swiftly she opened the collar on Louise's dress and lowered her carefully to the floor. Grabbing the phone, she dialed the emergency number listed on the directory.

Voice trembling, she gave the necessary information to the ambulance service. Hanging the phone up, Jaycee knelt and raised Louise's limp wrist.

"Weak," she said, finding the pulse, "but there."

Only minutes later two men in white uniforms hustled into the small office with a stretcher. Jaycee could taste the tears when she said, "Don't let her die. Please. Don't let her die."

Efficiently the attendants moved Louise onto the stretcher, placing a portable oxygen mask over her face. At full speed they wheeled the patient out the front door.

"You coming?" one attendant shouted over his shoulder.

Climbing into the back of the ambulance, she saw the doors slam, heard the siren wail, felt the jolt of the speeding vehicle, but none of it seemed real.

"Hang in there, lady," she heard the attendant say. Jaycee didn't know wheither he was speaking to Louise or to herself. *Don't die, Louise,* was the only thought on her mind. Jaycee held the older woman's wrinkled, blue-veined hand. Her fingertips were beginning to feel cool.

The short trip to the city hospital took minutes, but seemed like endless hours. Each second was precious. Standing aside as they wheeled the stretcher into the emergency room, Jaycee mumbled, "I never told her how much I love her."

Seconds slowly ticked away, becoming minutes. Minutes dragged into an hour. Pacing the floor,

Jaycee wrung her hands. She had had the presence of mind to call Louise's son, Robert. They were on their way. They hadn't asked what had caused the attack and Jaycee hadn't told them. She blamed herself. If she had reassured Louise instead of drilling her with questions, she wouldn't be dying in a hospital.

"If only . . ." *If only.*

The double doors swung open into the waiting room.

"Doctor?" Jaycee said, not wanting to ask.

"If she makes it through the next twenty-four hours, she should have a full recovery. Right now she's in intensive care in the cardiac section. We're keeping a close eye on her just as a precaution. That's all I can tell you now."

"Can I see her?" Jaycee asked, wanting to see for herself that Louise was going to live.

"Not now," the doctor answered, shaking his head. In a kind voice, he added, "Maybe later, after she's out of intensive care."

"She means so much to me. She's like a mother." Jaycee felt the need to justify the request. The guilt she felt clung to her as heavy as a winter coat.

"I'll let you know if there is any change. How are you feeling? Do you need something to calm your nerves?" Keen medical eyes did a quick perusal.

"No. I don't need anything. Just take care of Louise."

Giving her a slow smile, he patted her shoulder with understanding and left the waiting room.

Relief was gradually replacing Jaycee's fear as the

doctor's words sank in. And knowing the chances of full recovery were possible lightened the load of guilt she carried.

Louise had taken the only option available. No malice had been intended. Bob had needed money desperately and his grandmother had supplied it. Pride, shame, and ignorance had kept the money from being replaced.

There had been clues during the past few years indicating Louise's unusual frugality. Jaycee remembered giving her a Christmas bonus and telling her to buy a new, bright red dress for the annual company Christmas party. Louise hadn't. When asked why, the older woman had shrugged and told her she didn't want to look like Mrs. Santa Claus.

I should have known, Jaycee berated herself. *All the signs were there; I didn't see them.*

The double doors hurled open. Louise's son, Robert, his wife, Missy, and their son, Bob, strode hurriedly into the room.

"How is she?" Robert asked with concern.

"If she makes it through the next twenty-four hours, she'll be okay."

A collective sigh of relief passed through the family's lips. Robert and Bob were dressed for work in jeans and short-sleeved plaid shirts. They had forgotten to remove the carpenter's hammers that hung in the loops at the sides of their upper thighs. Missy was in a misbuttoned housedress.

"Thank God," Missy said gratefully.

After they all sat down, Jaycee gave them an edited edition of what had happened in the office. Bob's unshed tears made his eyes shimmer. Before they could dart away from Jaycee's face, she saw the guilt in them. When she finished speaking, she caught his eye again.

Blue eyes, much like his grandmother's, were imploring. *What?* Then she knew. Bob's parents didn't know about the money. He didn't want them to find out now. Nodding her head, she agreed to keep the secret. She owed that to Louise.

"If you'll excuse me, I have a couple of calls to make," Jaycee told Louise's family.

Bob followed Jaycee out into the hallway on the pretext of going for coffee.

"You know, don't you?"

"I know," Jaycee answered succinctly.

"This is all my fault. Granny could have died because of me." Bob slammed his fist into his palm.

The twenty-year-old's reaction surprised Jaycee. He had automatically assumed her guilt. The unshed tears were now coursing down his face, his shoulders racked with sobs. Stepping close, Jaycee held him like an injured child, shushing his tears. It took several minutes for Bob to get himself under control. Rubbing his eyes with his fist, he boyishly wiped his nose on his sleeve.

"You're not responsible," Jaycee lied. If the worst did happen, Jaycee didn't want Louise's favorite grandson to carry the burden of guilt. "Your grandmother told me about the money last Thursday. The CPA can handle it."

"But the money is in Granny's savings account. Did you get it?"

141

"It's all taken care of." She lied again. Giving him a sisterly poke on the arm, she said, "Go wash your face and get some coffee." Turning away, she started toward the phone booth.

"Jaycee?"

Pivoting, she saw a weak smile on Bob's face.

"Thanks. I'm sorry if I got you in trouble."

Waving a hand in friendly dismissal, she headed back toward the phone booth. Calling the office first, she told one of the foremen to stick around for repair calls and instructed him on what the other crews were to complete. The second call was to Scotty. Briefly she explained where she was and what had happened.

"Are the files still on your desk?"

"They should be."

"I'll go over to the office, pick them up, and see what I can do. This is going to be rough without having the money. I'd offer to loan it to you, but, frankly, I don't have that amount either."

"I know you would. Do your best," she said, touched by the offer to use his own personal funds.

"Are you going to stay at the hospital?"

"Yes. Louise is more important right now than anything."

"Okay. I'll call later tonight when I know what's going on. Give her family my love."

Resting her head in the corner of the phone booth, Jaycee twisted the length of her ponytail. She had done this often as a child, seldom as an adult. Being vulnerable made old habits resurface. Louise had

142

once told her that she was lucky. She had "home-grown" worry beads.

Hours later the family was allowed to peek into the intensive care room. Jaycee paced from one end of the waiting room to the other while they were gone. Missy came back crying. Seeing Louise helpless and frail in an oxygen tent was frightening. The danger period hadn't passed. There was still a risk.

After a dinner that none of them ate, the small group returned for the long night's vigil. None of them went home. Hourly they asked for reports. The answer was the same: vital signs holding.

The agony of waiting was made wholly frustrating by being unable to reach Scotty. He was either out or the phone was busy. Jonathan couldn't be reached either. It was as though the whole world had closed up shop and left Jaycee in a sterile hospital.

Robert and Bob dozed off and on in the upright chairs lining the wall. Jaycee and Missy tried to sleep on the short sofas. Strangers, absorbed in their own emergencies, drifted in and out of the waiting room. Each time the door opened, four pairs of eyes watched for a nurse or doctor assigned to Louise's case.

Three nights with little sleep, added to the worry and discomfort of being at the hospital, were taking their toll on Jaycee. At daybreak, exhausted from mental and emotional strain, her body took over. The sleep that had been elusive overcame the strong will to stay awake.

"Jaycee. Wake up. Louise wants to see you."

The quiet, even tones of the doctor immediately made the reserve adrenaline flow.

"Is she better?" Jaycee asked, rubbing the red eyes underlined by dark circles.

"She's restless. Your name is constantly on her lips," he informed her. "Whatever is bothering her, you must eliminate it. Can you do it? Calmly?"

Thrusting her chin forward, nodding her head, Jaycee walked briskly down the hall with the tall, lean doctor. Bone weary, she knew it would take a great measure of self-control not to break down in front of Louise.

"In here," the doctor said, pointing toward an open door.

Settling herself in a chair at the bedside, she said softly, "Louise. I'm here."

Louise's hand rose slightly, then fell back onto the starched white sheet. Leaning closer to the oxygen tent, Jaycee saw her mouth the word *purse*.

"I'll bring it to you, dear. Don't worry about it."

The limp hand moved in agitation. She watched her lips move again. No sound could be heard.

"Slip?" Jaycee's dark eyes pierced the plastic enclosure. "Pink slip?"

Her nod was practically nonexistent.

"I'll take care of it. Stop worrying."

Louise visibly relaxed, falling into a peaceful slumber. Jaycee watched the doctor and nurse reading the complicated machinery attached to Louise. Their low voices were indistinct. Silently the doctor gestured for Jaycee to leave the room.

"Her blood pressure was dropping back into the high normal range. Your being there was more effective than any medication we've given her." Once again his eyes swept over her. "You'd better go home and rest or I'll have two patients," he said gruffly. "The crisis period is over. She'll make it."

Jaycee felt as though a heavy load of pipe had been removed from her shoulders. "Thanks, Doctor. I'll tell the family."

On the way back downstairs Jaycee puzzled over the importance of bringing Louise's purse and a pink slip to the hospital. She's probably worried about money for so long, Jaycee reasoned, she didn't want to be anywhere without her purse. That was understandable. But why did she need a pink slip? Did she sleep in a slip rather than a nightgown? Too exhausted to solve the puzzle and eager to impart the good news, she rushed out of the elevator toward the waiting room.

Half an hour later Bob pulled up in front of her house. As he helped her out of the car, Jaycee saw Jonathan charging down the front steps. Bob's arm protectively circled her slender, drooping shoulders. Seeing the anger blazing from gray slits, she shook the arm off and stepped between the two men.

"Bob is Louise's son. She had a heart attack," she explained quickly before Jonathan could say or do anything. The fire was doused immediately.

"I've been sick with worry," he said, crushing her into his arms.

"I'm going back to the hospital," she heard Bob say.

Yawning, she replied sleepily, "See you later."

Resting against Jonathan's strength, Jaycee allowed herself to be led up the front steps. Handing Jonathan the key, she leaned against the doorjamb while he unlocked and opened it. Seeing her state of complete exhaustion, he gently lifted her into his arms.

"Upstairs?"

"Umm-hmm," she yawned. Keeping her eyes open was taking altogether too much effort. Snuggling her head against Jonathan's muscular chest, she fell asleep.

The sun was streaming in her westerly window when she began to stir. The hunger gnawing at the pit of her stomach made it growl loudly.

"Sounds as though the big ones are eating the little ones," she mumbled. Yawning, stretching, she turned the bedclothes back. She was naked as a newborn babe. Brown eyes popped open.

"Jonathan," she said softly out loud. Her rumpled clothes were neatly draped over the blue velvet occasional chair. On the night table, propped up against the phone, was a note in bold cursive. It read:

> Temptress!
> You begged prettily for me to stay,
> but I had to change and go to work.
> Call *before* you go to the shop.
> Jonathan

Smiling, she put the note on the night table. She dialed information and asked for the hospital number.

"City Hospital. May I help you?"

"Could you tell me the conditon of Louise White?"

"Satisfactory."

"Thank you. Bye."

Pressing the button, she disconnected the line. The dial tone buzzed in her ear before she punched the next number into the receiver.

"Scotty?"

"Yes, Jaycee," he answered, recognizing her voice. "How's Louise?"

"Stable. I just woke up. Do you know anything yet?"

Scotty paused. Jaycee could hear him flipping through papers. Good news travels fast. The pause lengthened. Intuitively she knew Scotty was trying to figure out the most tactful means of relaying the bad news.

"Jaycee, is there any way you can get your hands on that amount fast?

"Not unless I rob a bank or several filling stations," she answered glibly, hoping humor would postpone the impending disaster.

"Did you go through the files before Louise had her attack?"

"No."

"Well, I have. Louise must have made some promises on the telephone too. You say she has the money?"

"Yes. In a saving account. But I don't know where."

The full importance of her lack of immediate funds was finally hitting her. Stomach twisting, she knew Scotty couldn't help her. Without the cash, the padlock was inevitable.

"Unless I can take a cashier's check to the IRS office, my hands are tied. I'm sorry."

"Me too. Maybe Jonathan can figure out a way to postpone the action. Thanks anyway, Scotty. Bye."

When it rains, it pours, had never been truer. How was she going to get out of this? Could Jonathan use his influence? He was her only hope, the single ray of sunlight shining on a gloomy day.

The doorbell ringing brought her from the depths of what was rapidly nearing despair. Slipping on a cotton coverup, she ran down the carpeted steps. The ring was persistent. Using the peephole, Jaycee saw Jonathan's back. Long fingers were raking through his blond hair.

"I was getting ready to phone you, Jonathan. Come in off the porch," she invited cordially.

As the door shut, Jaycee wrapped her arms around his neck. Soundly she kissed him on the lips. No response. This was hardly the reaction she expected from the man who had been beside himself last night. A cold, marble statue would have been as warm. *Try, try, try again,* she thought.

Gently she nibbled at the corner of his lower lip.

148

He had liked that. Hadn't he told her he did? Why was he tensing up?

"What's wrong?" she asked, knowing the answer before he spoke.

"Do you want it straight or shall I sweeten it first?" he asked stiffly.

"Straight." The monosyllable nearly stuck in her throat. She didn't want to hear what he was going to tell her. The drone in his voice was the same tone she'd heard the first day they had met.

"Larry Dettrick and I are on the way to the shop." The level, penetrating look he shot Jaycee didn't leave room for doubt.

Fighting the urge to cover her ears, Jaycee turned, slowly walking away. "Larry need another thingumabob?" she asked with a weak laugh.

Moving toward her, the distance between them remained static; Jaycee was taking two small steps backward for his one step forward until her back was against the papered wall.

"Isn't there anything you can do? Work something out with Scotty? Talk to your boss?" The questions were asked in a flat voice.

"I've talked to Scott several times. He told me about Louise and the money." One hand rubbed over his forehead as though he had a severe headache.

All Jaycee's strength was being used to remain calm. The man she loved, had made passionate love to, was going to put her out of business. How could he do it? *No heart,* she thought miserably. If he had any compassion, he'd light a match to the buildings rather than forbid her entry.

149

Stepping away from the wall, she wound her arms around his waist. "Please, Jonathan. Help me."

"I've tried everything." His arms wrapped around her shoulders. Burying his face in her hair, she felt him tremble.

"Lose the papers. Tell them you put the padlock on, but don't." She hated begging. Even worse, she hated using his love for her as a weapon. It was wrong and she knew it. She couldn't stop the illegal suggestions. For too long the plumbing business had been her life. Anything short of violence was justifiable.

"I can't. Don't ask it." The rejection was muffled as it came from beneath her loose, uncombed hair.

"If you love me . . ."

Woman's oldest, most used bargaining tools were halted by Jonathan's hand clamping over her lips. "Don't." The moistness from her lips was wiped on his suit pants. That gesture said everything and nothing. "I have to go. Larry is waiting in the car." Shoulders slumped slightly, he headed for the door.

Jaycee froze. She regretted having tried to exchange love for a padlock. Every bone, muscle, organ, in her body hurt. The pain of knowing her business was flushing down the tubes, and being helpless to prevent it was tearing her limb from limb.

"Dinner is off?" she asked coldly, wanting to have the final word.

The question went unanswered. Not looking back, Jonathan walked out the door. He had not removed himself from the case as promised, only from her life.

150

Heartless son-of-a-biscuit-eater, she cursed silently. The altered cursing rang out coarsely in her mind. Harsh laughter followed. *Stupid female fool,* she chastized herself. The one thing Jonathan couldn't *take* from her she had wantonly given.

Determined steps led her to the living room phone. Punching out the office number in quick jabs, she waited for the call to be completed.

"Bud? Listen carefully. Grab the company checkbook and the black business directory. Take the new van and go straight home. I'll explain later."

"But . . . there won't be anyone left in the shop."

"Never mind the shop. Oh, yes. Get Louise's purse out of her bottom drawer. She's worried about it. Thanks, Bud. I'll meet you at your place."

Returning the receiver to its holder, she placed her fist over her mouth, squeezing both lips between thumb and folded fingers. Logically, systematically, Jaycee considered her options. If Louise survived, it was only a matter of a few days before the money would be available. The trucks would have to return to the shop, but not the complete inventory. The men could partially transfer the equipment and fittings they needed into their own vehicles. She could do that herself. Better, she thought. *If it's illegal, I'll be the only one responsible.*

Next, call the suppliers and contractors. The company's reputation was strong. Calling before they heard it through the grapevine would add some psychological advantage.

Checking her watch, she rushed up the steps.

151

Making those phonecalls was top priority, but first she'd have to get to Bud's house. Four hours to save the business. The race against time would be the biggest obstacle.

Half an hour later Jaycee paced the sidewalk in front of Bud's house. Dark eyes made bright by the challenge in front of her were glued to the direction of the shop.

"Come on, Bud," she chanted repeatedly.

A Jaycee Plumbing van rounded the corner on two wheels. Waving her hands frantically, she signaled for Bud to stop in front rather than pull the van to the back of the house. Tires screeched on the hot pavement.

"Give me the directory, checkbook, and purse. Back the van up to the trunk of my car." The instructions were issued forcefully and concisely.

Minutes later half of the contents of the van were crammed into the trunk and back seat of her car, and she had explained the situation to Bud. They mutually decided to divide the job sites and inform the men. Jaycee would contact the large jobs; Bud would inform the men on the smaller sites. Bud assured her the loyalty built up over the years would generate enough trust to keep the men from walking off the job.

"Darn. I've got to call the bank."

Spotting a public phone, she swerved to the curb. On the run, Jaycee emptied her pockets. Bess, the bank teller, would discreetly check the company account.

"Bess Parker, please," she informed the switchboard operator.

"Bess? Jaycee Warner. Would you check the status of the business account please?" The short metal phone cord restricted her movement like a leash.

"It is," Jaycee said dispiritedly. The account was frozen. Company funds would not be available. "Thanks, Bess."

Scratch cashing a payroll check from the list. Jogging back to the car, she climbed in and threw it into gear. When the car pulled into the parking lot of the ten-story job site, she beeped the signal. Climbing out of the van, she paced, organizing her thoughts.

"Hi, Boss Lady. What brings you down here?" the middle-aged, baldheaded foreman asked.

"Trouble! Spelled I-R-S. Leave the tools, fittings, and copper in the job trailer tonight. Tell the men to be at my house right after work."

"That's tough. Did you call your old man?" A worried frown creased the face of Jack Benson, her lead foreman.

The first sign of trouble and Ben wanted a man at the helm. That rankled.

"I can take care of the business," Jaycee replied curtly.

"You're taking a chance leaving the power tools in the trailer. Every thief in the downtown area will be headed over here."

"Hide them under the fittings and plywood. When you bring them out of the building have them *in* something."

The foreman shook his bald head. "They'll be stolen for sure. I'll take them home with me."

Raising her eyes to the man who had first taught her how to solder, she smiled. "You're asking for trouble with Uncle Sam."

"Time to close ranks to outsiders." Tugging her ponytail, he added, "Can't let the best lady plumber in town go out of business."

The burden of carrying her problems alone was being lifted, shared. Beaming him a wide smile, she quipped with her usual spunkiness, "The *only* lady plumber in town."

"Get out of here, kid," he replied with friendly gruffness. "I've got a job to run. No time to make copper guns."

The revival of a lost memory caused a lump to lodge in her throat. Jack had made a replica of a space gun for her eighth birthday, combining a mixture of half-inch copper and fittings. The gleaming gun was the envy of every boy on the block. When she had imperiously demanded he make more guns, he'd sternly told her to make them herself. Ben supervised the project. When she assembled the gun without cleaning the fittings, he had exploded, shouting, "Union plumbers clean *every* fitting." Stomping her foot, she'd screamed, "I'm not a union plumber. I'm a *kid!*" The childish tantrum won her a swift swat on the rear end, a severe shake, and the statement, "You will be." Sniffling, she had pulled the gun apart and cleaned the copper and the fittings. The lesson was well learned. As a union plumber she seldom had a water leak, and if she did, it was never due to dirty fittings.

"Clean your fittings," she croaked past the lump. Ducking her head, she climbed back into the car.

Twenty-three hot, sweaty plumbers faced Jaycee. Respectfully they hushed their conversations when she stepped on the back porch. Most of them knew the problem. A red sticker on the shop door explained it all.

Clearing her throat, Jaycee began, "How do you feel about using your vacation stamps?"

The question was met by dead silence.

"No!" Jack shouted loudly.

The others joined in, giving a negative reply.

Both callused hands rose and she quieted the crews. "That was one choice. The other is risky." Her voice was loud enough to be heard, but held a calm, authoritative quality. "The company bank account is temporarily frozen." Groans could be heard coming from the newer employees. "There is every possibility you will *not* be paid Friday."

"Who's got our money?" she heard from the back of the group.

Jaycee tried to attach the voice to a face and couldn't.

"The bank has frozen the account under court order from the IRS." Thrusting her chin, she asked the question that would seal the fate of the company. "Will you take a chance on me? I promise you will get your paychecks a week from Friday if I have to beg, borrow, or steal the money."

155

The group was completely silent. Jack stepped forward.

"We discussed our options before the meeting. We'll stick." The men roared approval. Reaching into his shirt pocket, he pulled out a green check. "This won't take care of your problem, but it should cover the cost of supplies for the week."

Jaycee was stunned. Company loyalty was one thing, but for her men to donate money to keep her shop open was another. That was the most touching gesture possible. Tears coursed down her cheeks unchecked. Bending her head, she swiped at them with the backs of her hands.

Placing the check in her hand, Jack said quietly, "We trust you with our jobs and our savings accounts. Read the note."

"Keep the huckleberries off Jaycee," she read softly. A broad smile slashed her face. Huckleberries were lumps of solder that ran down the shiny copper when the joints were full. A good plumber always wiped them off.

A roar of male laughter broke the silence. Jaycee wrapped her arms around Jack's neck. He swung her around twice, then put her feet firmly on the ground. Jaycee began shaking hands with each member of the crew. Most of them tried to wipe the grime and flux, embedded from a day's work, on their work pants. Jaycee laughed. What was a little dirt among friends?

"Keep the huckleberries off Jaycee," was murmured time and time again.

"Men," Jack said after Jaycee had thanked each of

156

them individually, "we all have to go home and explain to our wives and girl friends why we gave our money to a cute blonde. If any of you need Dutch courage, I'll buy you a beer at John's."

The announcement was met with a boisterous cheer and a thunderous clapping of hands.

"Thanks again," Jaycee shouted, clutching the check in her hands. The men had proven themselves to be the light at the end of a dark, lonely tunnel.

Parking the car across from the hospital, Jaycee picked up both purses and hurriedly strode toward the hospital entrance. Bob met her halfway up the stone steps.

"Why did you lie to me, Jaycee?" he demanded abruptly.

"Lie?"

"You told me you had the money and the CPA was taking care of everything. I drove by the shop after talking to Granny, and it was locked up." His hand raked over his head, pushing an errant lock back in place. "Did you get the money? Don't lie again," he warned.

"No. It's still in her savings account."

"Why didn't you go to the bank and get the money?" he asked persistently.

"Because I needed her signature."

"Granny said she . . ." Bob plucked her purse from under Jaycee's arm. Opening it, he rifled through the contents. A pink piece of paper was held between his fingers and waved under her nose. "Purse. Pink slip.

Granny said those words, didn't she?"

Jaycee realized the pink paper fluttering before her was the pink slip—a signed withdrawal form. If she hadn't been exhausted, she would have decoded the message herself.

"I have to get to a phone. Come on!"

CHAPTER NINE

CPA and client waited in the large Internal Revenue Service office. Typewriters clickity-clacked as letters and forms were completed by the clerks. Small offices lined the outer wall of the open typing pool. A series of small booths edged the opposite wall.

"Mr. Dettrick will see you now. Last office on your right."

Glancing down, Jaycee picked an imaginary piece of lint off her navy blue business suit. Only the white ruffled blouse relieved the stark lines. Long hair French-plaited, makeup appropriate for daytime wear, high heels making her slender legs appear longer, Jaycee felt confident of her appearance. Only the tight hold on her purse betrayed the cool façade.

Larry and Jonathan stood politely as she entered the office. Scotty shook hands with both men, then courteously seated Jaycee. The office was crowded with two steel desks back to back and the two straight clients chairs.

Scotty handed Jonathan the cashier's check. Tension strung between the two men as tight as a plumb bob.

"I believe this will cover the delinquent taxes plus interest," Scott said coolly.

The check was passed to Agent Dettrick. Shuffling through a stack of papers, he extracted a release form. Scott skimmed the paper, folded it, and inserted it in his breast pocket.

Brown eyes met bright silver eyes. *He looks like hell,* Jaycee thought. Her face was equally ravaged, but fortunately she could cover the damage with blusher and base coat. *You hurt me,* Jaycee telepathed. Jonathan shook his head as he received the message.

"When will the company bank account be released?" Back to business, she thought. Personal problems could be sorted out later. Payday was Friday. If humanly possible, the men would not miss a paycheck.

"It should be released immediately," Larry answered. "I'll personally call the bank."

"Then it's wrapped up?" Scotty asked, standing.

"Should be. If you have any problems, call." Larry rose to his feet. "Jaycee, thanks again for the . . . ah . . ."

"Adapter," Jaycee said, suppling the proper term. Gracefully she arose from the uncomfortable chair. A twinkle entered her eyes. "Don't call the competitors"—her head tilted slightly toward Jonathan—"for a plugged-up john." Pasting a serene, placid mask on her face, she turned to Jonathan. She avoided touching his outstretched hand. "Good-bye, Mr. Wynthrop. Our business is finished."

Shoving his empty hand into his pocket, he said,

"I'll walk you to your car. I'm on my way to Washington University." Before she could object, she felt strong fingers clamped over her elbow. "I'm late for a lecture."

Jaycee saw him shoot a fierce look at Scotty. It wasn't necessary. Scotty was grinning from ear to ear. Larry's wink was a carbon copy of Jonathan's. *Men! No matter whose side they started on, when the final countdown came, they hung together.*

"We need to talk," Jonathan said after they were out of the office and waiting for the elevator.

"Mr. Wynthrop," Jaycee answered calmly, even though her heart was thudding in her chest, "you said it all . . . yesterday."

"I'll pick you up for dinner," he stated with determination.

"I'll be with Louise at the hospital."

"Then I'll pick you up after visiting hours."

Stepping into the elevator, she slapped her purse against her upper thigh. "Is this really necessary, Mr. Wynthrop?"

"Yes, damn it, it is." The question strained his patience and temper.

The elevator doors closed. The slowly descending room provided intimate seclusion. Jonathan's expensive aftershave filled Jaycee's nostrils. Her back itched. A light spell of dizziness made her lean against the back wall.

"No, *darn* it. It isn't. When I needed you, begged for your help, you weren't available."

"You didn't beg, you bargained. There is one *hell* of a difference."

"The end result would have been the same. And quit cursing around me, Mr. Wynthrop."

"One more 'Mr. Wynthrop' and I'll throttle her," Jonathan muttered under his breath.

It is childish to be so formal, she thought, studying his face. Lines made a deep groove beside his tautly compressed lips. Thumb and fingertips rubbed over the parallel wrinkles on his forehead. What devious plan is next, she wondered. If he didn't touch her, she knew she could sustain the ladylike façade.

The doors opened. Jaycee's high heels clicked on the marble floor.

"You don't know all the facts," he stated, pushing a cuff back and glancing at his watch. "Read the release form carefully," he advised.

Not waiting for a reply, he sprinted down the sidewalk. Rounding the corner to the underground parking garage, he paused, grinned, and waved.

Biting her tongue was the only thing keeping her from calling him back. The physical pain hurt less than the mental anguish she had been through. He had fooled her once. The facts were simple and plain. Jaycee Warner had fallen in love with Jonathan Wynthrop. The feelings weren't mutual or he would have helped her. *Never again,* she vowed.

Two months later Louise was back at work and Jaycee was compiling the weekly supply lists. Labor Day weekend was approaching and she wanted to clear the business litter off her desk.

Time was healing the hurt and shame. Days were no longer filled with thoughts and images of Jonathan. The long hours she worked usually meant she was too exhausted to remember the dreams. His phone calls remained unanswered. The phone had rung constantly the first few days, but over the weeks they had dwindled and finally stopped.

The "IRS Disaster," as Louise called it, actually had a few positive results. Jaycee was more confident in the role of employer and the barriers that had kept her from dating had been thoroughly destroyed.

After considerable prompting from Louise, she had accepted a date with a general contractor. Hank was attractive, attentive, had a good sense of humor. Why couldn't she deepen the relationship? Something, some magical ingredient, was missing.

Restlessly Jaycee tapped the eraser end of the pencil on the checkbook. Jonathan had subtly invaded her thoughts. *Darn it! There are too many unanswered questions.* The chair creaked as she leaned back. She'd read and reread that release a thousand times. It was a standard fill-in-the-blank form. What did he mean by "you don't know all the facts?"

None of the pieces to the puzzle fit. Wondering, speculating, hypothesizing, made the picture fuzzier. It was time for action, she decided, picking up the phone.

Dialing Jonathan's home number, she held her breath, then released it heavily when she heard a recorded message. Sighing deeply, she put the phone down. The chair groaned as she lowered it. Was she glad or disappointed that she didn't talk to him? Both emotions were weirdly mixed together.

Reaching down, Jaycee opened her bottom desk

drawer and pulled out a can of all-purpose oil. After several squirts in strategic spots, she leaned back. No groan. No creak. A broad smile split her lips. Why hadn't she done something about that ages ago, she thought.

"Louise, do you still have the morning paper?"

"By the coffeepot, dear."

On page ten of the entertainment section she found what she was searching for: a list of free lectures at the local colleges. Jonathan Wynthrop, tax attorney, she read silently, Small Businesses and the IRS, Thursday, 7:00 P.M. Reception following.

"Mind if I leave the closing-up for you today, Louise?" she asked, making a decision.

"Big date?"

"No. A business meeting." The answer was evasive but true.

"You run along. I'll lock up," Louise said with a knowing smile.

The auditorium was cool and dimly lit. Hushed expectancy was in the air. Seated halfway between the front and back of the large plush lecture hall, Jaycee felt safe. It was one thing to satisfy the whim to solve the pieces of a puzzle, but quite another to be discovered. Darkness provided anonymity.

The campus clock chimed seven times just as Jonathan walked to the podium. A spotlight from the balcony caught the shine of the golden streaks in his hair, its bright intensity changing the lighter strands to silver.

Flashing a smile to the audience, he welcomed

164

them warmly. Jaycee was stunned by her own reaction at seeing him. *Surprise?* Why should she be surprised at his being as fit and handsome as he had ever been? Did she expect to see a shriveled-up, malnourished, broken-hearted man? He hadn't aged one bit.

When his speech began she didn't comprehend the words. The husky tenor quality of his voice brought back memories she knew were best buried. The tiny smile turning her lips upward was quickly covered by her hand. Each time Jonathan gestured she remembered the feel of his hands touching her. Closing her eyes, she could visualize those same long fingers caressing her from shoulder to thigh, the way his dark tan contrasted sharply with the creamy white skin normally hidden by clothes. How many times had he wrapped her hair around his wrist? Inwardly she groaned. *This must stop,* she reprimanded herself.

The people surrounding Jaycee laughed. She heard Jonathan's projected chuckle and saw his lips spread into a wide grin. The charisma that first attracted Jaycee had the same effect on the audience. The elderly lady on her right sighed deeply. Sitting up straight, Jaycee pulled herself out of the erotic reverie and tried to appear interested but not overly enthralled.

At the end of the lecture the houselights were turned back up. The older lady next to her stood up. A microphone was passed from the aisle down the row. Jaycee had the urge to slump or bend over, but didn't.

"Young man, you seem to be a nice-enough

youngster." The audience laughed. "Didn't it bother you to literally end the monetary aspirations of small businessmen?"

Breathing deeply, Jaycee awaited his answer. Gray eyes dropped slightly. An electrical current seemed to pass from the podium to the middle of the auditorium. She tingled from head to toe from the voltage.

"IRS agents have a thankless job. Dracula on a moonlit night gets a heartier welcome."

The lady questioner nodded her head, twittering.

"But does it bother them? Yes! Constantly being a villain takes its toll. You must have a healthy ego to step back and realize the anger and bitterness is not directed *personally* at the agent doing his job."

Jaycee schooled the expression on her face to remain serene. Knowing the question was answered with her case in mind, she tried objectively to interpret the hidden meaning. Other clients might not personally reject the agent, but by refusing his phonecalls she certainly had. Separating one's life from one's livelihood was easier said than done. She hadn't been able to do it.

"What about bribery? Did you get any offers?"

Jaycee shifted forward in her seat. Other members of the audience whispered nervously to each other. The total atmosphere became tense.

"Bribery takes many forms. Not all of them are illegal. How many of you have given your child a piece of candy at the checkout line in a grocery store?"

Several hands rose. Others clapped. Jonathan smiled.

"Anyone *pay* for good grades?" He chuckled as the applause became louder. "That is bribery!" Almost everyone laughed. "Anyone ever start a sentence with 'If you love me . . . ?" His head swiveled toward Jaycee. "That, too, is bribery."

Jaycee cringed. Had silver-gray eyes branded a big B on her forehead? She wanted to get up and walk out, but couldn't.

Continuing, Jonathan turned toward the man who asked the question. "Bribery can be subtle or blatant. That is why agents travel in pairs. It keeps them honest and . . . they avoid falling into foolish traps."

The president of the college joined Jonathan at the podium. Shaking hands and smiling, he thanked Jonathan for an informative, entertaining lecture and invited the audience to enjoy refreshments at the reception immediately following the lecture.

Starting up the main aisle, Jonathan received a standing ovation. This was partially a matter of campus etiquette, but was due mostly to his popularity. Rising to her feet, Jaycee stood, politely clapping.

"Isn't he wonderful?" the older woman said to no one in particular.

Long athletic strides swiftly brought Jonathan closer and closer to the row Jaycee occupied. He paused, looked at Jaycee, and winked. Not a quick, I-see-you wink, but a slow, sensuous lowering of one eyelid.

The older lady squeaked, "Oh! Did you see him

wink at me? I can hardly wait to get to the reception."

Gradually the large group of people began heading toward the main exit. Smiling, Jaycee ignored being pressed aside by women anxious to meet Jonathan. The pieces to the puzzle hadn't been solved, but she had gained insight into the choices forced upon Jonathan. All in all, she was glad she had attended the lecture.

Stepping through the double doors, she was surprised when she felt a hand at her elbow.

"Enjoy the lecture? Or the lecturer?"

"Well. Hello, Scotty. Long time no see. How's Ruth?"

"Vacationing in Mexico. Want to take pity on your best friend's fiancé, not to mention your own devoted CPA, and grab a bite to eat?"

"I'd love it." She accepted enthusiastically.

The large majority of the people were turning left to the reception area. In companionable silence Jaycee and Scotty went out the huge, heavily carved doors leading outside.

Jonathan was waiting at the bottom of the steps. Gray eyes, filled with admiration and amusement, followed her descending path. The crinkles fanning the corners of his eyes indicated . . . what? Delight at seeing her?

"Scotty . . . Jaycee. Good to see you." Jonathan's gray eyes never left her face. The feminine yellow cotton sundress with matching jacket outlined her figure as the evening breeze made the soft fabric cling, the billow against her legs. The gray eyes told her silently that she was stunning.

"Good speech, Jonathan. Made me feel more compassionate toward IRS agents," Scotty joked.

"Are you feeling compassionate?" Jonathan huskily asked Jaycee.

"Confused," she replied honestly.

"Aren't you the guest of honor at the reception?" Scotty asked, noticing two of the ushers walking purposefully toward them.

Turning in the direction Scotty was facing, Jaycee heard him mutter a mild expletive.

"Won't you two join me?

"No, thanks," Jaycee replied quickly before Scotty could accept the invitation. "The lady sitting next to me . . . the one you winked at"—she explained with false innocence—"is anxiously awaiting your arrival."

"You could come and defend my honor," he teased.

"That's one of the things I'm confused about."

"Mr. Wynthrop, pardon me for interrupting, but there's a pack of women ready to riot in the reception room. Would you please come with us?" The expression the youth wore was one of pure, unadulterated hero worship.

"Scotty, would you excuse us for a moment?" Jonathan asked, turning Jaycee toward the steps. "Walk with me."

Climbing the steps, Jaycee noticed the two young men were following as close as puppy dogs. A strange mixture of disappointment and relief blended together. The magical spell she'd been under in the auditorium was distorting reality. Now wasn't the time for clear, logical thinking or reacting.

"Will you have a midnight dinner with me?" he asked in a soft, seductive voice.

"I seem to recall you have difficulty keeping dinner engagements." The past was not forgotten . . . or forgiven.

"You could fix breakfast for me," he coaxed, remembering another breakfast, served in bed.

The college boys behind them were stifling giggles unsuccessfully. Jonathan's eyes snapped in their direction. "Gentlemen. The lessons were in the building. Not out here. Move!"

Embarrassment tinged Jaycee's cheeks a delicate pink. The ushers scurried up the steps. They didn't want the wrath of their hero to fall on their shoulders. Jaycee didn't want it on hers either. This parting should be pleasant. A memory to treasure. One wiping away the guilt she felt over their last parting.

"It isn't that easy, Jonathan. Unfortunately we can't stop the clock at the lake and ignore everything else."

"Am I still the Dracula in that scenario?" His right hand jamming into his trouser pocket, his head down, he appeared to be studying her pink-tipped toes peeking out from the high-heeled sandals she wore. He removed his hand from his pocket and casually unbuttoned his suit jacket. Jaycee searched his eyes looking for . . . what? Tenderness? Passion? Love.

"Copper fires," he said, more to himself than to

170

Jaycee. The hand he'd used to undo his jacket trailed slowly down her back, settling on her belted waist.

Shivers went up her spine, raising goose bumps on her bare arms. Her resolves were weakening. Nothing seemed more important than wrapping herself around him and hanging on for dear life. *Stop! Stop! Stop!* the rational part of her mind screamed. *Remember . . . never again!*

Standing at the top of the steps, Jaycee glanced into the building. The ushers were ogling the scene. A look of expectation was on their faces.

"Come with me," he cajoled, his voice thick and heavy.

"I can't," she answered, shaking her head. A feeling of *déjà vu*, having been there before, swept between them. Those were the exact words he had used when denying her help.

"Mr. Wynthrop! They're coming!"

Twirling, Jaycee combined walking and skipping to get to the street level. Scotty was waiting. Refusing to glance over her shoulder for one last look, she took his arm and hurried Scotty down the sidewalk.

She knew her emotions were as mixed as the variety of fittings stocked at the shop. She needed to sort through them. Compartmentalize them. Find the important ones and put the rest back on the shelf.

Seated at a nearby campus Burger-doodle, she watched Scotty inhale two double cheeseburgers, a basket of french fries, and a large chocolate milkshake. The food in front of her was barely touched.

171

Conversation was limited by Scotty's mouth constantly being full.

Wiping his mouth on a paper napkin, he looked longingly at her hamburger. "Are you going to eat that or just pick it to death?"

"I'm not hungry."

"You see before you," he said in a courthouse tone, "two prime examples of dealing with misery. Sample one is labeled fat, the other skinny."

Jaycee couldn't help but chuckle at his foolishness.

Encouraged, Scotty continued, "Now I ask you, ladies and gentlemen of the jury, was it justifiable homicide?"

"You're going to bump off Ruth for making you miserably fat?" she asked, joining the repartee.

"No." Slapping his thigh, he laughed wickedly. "I have a more befitting justice in mind."

Lifting her eyebrow, Jaycee waited for the punch line.

"I'm going to kill her with love. By Christmas I'll be a mere shadow of my former self," he said, rubbing his paunch.

Playfully Jaycee reached over the table and pinched one chubby cheek. "Don't count on it."

Immediately sobering, he asked, "What do *you* count on these days?"

"My fingers and toes," she quipped, refusing to let the mood become serious.

Scotty guffawed at the unexpected response. "Come on, smart mouth. I'll walk you to your car."

Strolling back on campus, their conversation was punctuated with laughter. Safely installing her be-

172

hind the wheel of the car, Scotty leaned in the open window. "It won't fly, Jaycee. You have to finish one trip before you start another."

Perceptively she knew he was referring to Jonathan and her dates with the general contractor. "I know. That's why I came tonight. Just when I thought I had a handle on the right answers, Jonathan changed the questions."

Patting her shoulder, Scotty commiserated, "Hang in there, kid. Don't get lost in the shuffle. Bye."

Starting the car, Jaycee pulled out of the parking space and waved good night. Jonathan had said the last day they were together that he wasn't the type to get lost in the shuffle; but he had.

The conflict between his job and her business had finally driven them apart. The fears she had had that same morning had become a reality. When he couldn't . . . or wouldn't help keep the shop open, she had felt hurt and angry. Betrayed, she thought grimly. There must have been something he could have done. But what if there wasn't anything he could do? she argued mentally. What if he had done everything humanly possible?

"Agents are only human," she muttered. Word association brought her thinking to Jonathan's lecture. Flushing, she remembered the definition of bribery. Using "If you love me" was despicable. Being desperate didn't validate her behavior or excuse it. Should she apologize? Would that be the missing piece of the puzzle that was keeping her from moving on with her life?

Pulling the car into the detached garage, she cut the engine. *I'll call him first thing tomorrow and apologize.* Opening the car door and leaving the garage, she stared at the full moon bathing the backyard in moonlight. *No,* she decided, *I'll go see him on the way to the shop. The telephone is a cowardly device.*

Jaycee gasped in fright. A dark shadow was moving silently on the back porch. Spinning, she ran back toward the garage.

CHAPTER TEN

"Jaycee! It's me . . . Jonathan."

She stopped dead in her tracks. Turning, she pierced the darkness of the porch, trying to see him. Had her positive thought waves brought him? In her mind they had been together all evening.

Stepping out of the shadows into the sparse light, he said, "I didn't mean to frighten you. Who did you think was skulking around in your backyard?" He smiled broadly. "Dracula?"

"What are you doing here?" The inane question was out before she could control her mouth.

"Waiting to keep a dinner date," he answered softly.

You're two months too late almost popped out. Biting her tongue, she kept the impetuous words back.

"I've eaten. Would you settle for a cup of coffee and a sandwich?" she asked, closing the distance between them.

Jonathan chuckled. "That elicits a very trite response."

Cocking her head questioningly, she looked up at

Jonathan. He'd changed clothes. Gray slacks snuggly outlined his slim hips. A casual cotton knit shirt stretched over chest muscles and broad shoulders. The casual stance was concealing the dynamic energy she had witnessed in the lecture hall.

"In all the old movies the leading man embraces the woman and says, 'I'm hungry only for you,' and passionately kisses the leading lady." Dark shadows couldn't hide the bright sparks coming from his eyes. "If we go in that door . . ."

"How about the swing on the front porch?" she suggested, mentally agreeing with him. Going into the dark interior of her home was potentially dangerous. Desire for physical release from the ache below her stomach would lead them directly to her bedroom.

In single file they followed the narrow brick path to the spacious front porch. Steadying the swing until she was seated, Jonathan paused, then leaned against the railing.

"I miss you, Jaycee."

"I miss you too, Jonathan." Keeping her head lowered, she tried to sort through the myriad of emotions she was feeling. Happiness, dread, joy, sorrow, anticipation—all were mixed together. Most of all she had an intense longing to be held tenderly. "Won't you sit down?"

"Is that why you came to the lecture?" he asked, ignoring her request.

"Partially." How could she apologize with him the width of the porch away? Was he *trying* to be difficult? "Won't you please sit down." Jokingly she added the excuse, "I'll get a crick in my neck from you towering over me." A strained laugh indicated her discomfort.

Jonathan sank to his haunches. "You're safer with me over here," he responded flatly. His arms rested on his knees, fingers locked together, face upturned.

"Why did you come tonight?"

"I needed to solve a puzzle," she answered honestly. "And take some positive, forward steps in my life. I'd made up my mind to go see you in the morning," she admitted.

"Why?" he asked softly.

"I owe you an apology." In the filtered light, Jaycee saw the muscles in his arms tense. "The minute I began bargaining . . . what I felt for you . . . I knew I was wrong. Desperate, but wrong."

In one fluid motion Jonathan was on his feet and in the swing. Gently he picked up her hand and placed a kiss on each fingertip. No words could have been a sweeter acceptance. Turning her hand, he placed a moist kiss on the palm. Jaycee closed her fingers, savoring it.

"You've driven me crazy for two months," he said hoarsely. "You wouldn't return my calls. I even resorted to parking outside the shop to get a glimpse of you," he admitted. One arm reached over the back of the swing to encircle her shoulders.

Feeling the heat from his body and the smell of his woodsy cologne made Jaycee want to cuddle against his chest, but she restrained herself. "At first I didn't return your calls because I was furious. In the back of my mind I wanted you to hurt the way I did. The

the calls dwindled and stopped. That supported my theory about only being a holiday fling. I tried everything to stop thinking about you. Snapping a rubber band on my wrist every time you invaded my thoughts worked the best. I even dated another man."

Jonathan's fiddling with the hairpins holding the braids at the nape of her neck was causing her heart to beat erratically. The pins plinked one by one as they fell onto the wooden porch.

"I saw you leaving the shop with a tall, dark giant. I decided I'd been a fool. Here I was, mooning around like a lovesick kid, and you were out whooping it up."

Small hands leisurely crept up his chest to the streaked blond softness of his hair. Gently she shaped his head from the crown to the nape of his neck.

"Never a fool," she demurred. "Dating made the pain worse."

"I didn't even try that. You're everything I've wanted in a woman. Beautiful. Passionate. Bright. I've been in heaven and hell since we met." Having undone her braid, his fingers cupped her loosened hair, then her face. "I hurt myself more than I hurt you, love. When Larry put the lock on the door, I sat in the car in a catatonic state. That day I couldn't stop the wheels in motion."

"I know, love." Dark eyes saw the misery etched in the grooves beside his lips. Tenderly she felt herself enfolded in his arms. For the moment she was content to be held like a fragile piece of china. They had both suffered.

The porch swing swung gently, creaking with age. Katydids chirped from one end of the yard to the other, providing an outdoor symphony. Being together, holding each other, wasn't enough for any length of time. Their arms tightened in unison.

Jaycee tasted the cologne and the moisture that was uniquely Jonathan's. Arching her neck, she exposed the vein leading to her heart. His tender lips kissed the pulse point.

Moving to the center of the swing, Jonathan pulled Jaycee across his lap. Oblivious to the movement, she showered his closely shaven face with kisses from temple to chin and back again. Nibbling his lower lip the way she knew he liked brought erotic fingers circling her back, around her rib cage. "Kiss me, hon," she coaxed.

Lips closed, but not sealed, she moved them against his. Jonathan brushed aside the straps on her sundress, easing his fingers beneath the frothy lace strapless bra. Forefinger and thumb rolled the tip of her breast, making it peak. The tip of of her tongue darted past Jonathan's lips. Tasting the minty softness of his inner lip, she explored deeper as she had never done before. The hands that had held her tenderly now strained their bodies together.

She had been so wrong. As their tongues met she knew the misery they had been through was of her making. No man could make her feel this way. The shop, her work, everything she had thought was important, only marked time between their loving. She had bargained for her shop; she should have held tight to what they shared. His lips could have been salve soothing the injury. Never again would she reject anything he offered.

"Let me love you," she whispered against his mouth. "I need to be loved."

Masculine shoulders shuddering, his head lowered to her throat. Extracting his hand from the front of her dress, he slid it over her hip, down the length of her thigh. The silkiness of sheer panty hose enticed his hand beneath the hemline of her skirt. A flame of fire shot ahead of his fingers. Trying to control her breathing, she silently questioned, *Doesn't he know what he is doing to me? Is this a subtle torture? I want him so badly.*

"Jonathan?"

Wordlessly he stood, lifting her with him, and carried her to the front door. "It's unlocked," she whispered, draping her arms around his shoulders.

"Dangerous," he muttered. "You could be robbed . . . or worse."

"Promises, promises," she replied cheekily, nipping his earlobe. "Straight back . . . on your left."

Feet touching the carpet, she quickly shed her clothes, rejecting Jonathan's shaking fingers. Naked, eager, she slipped between the sweet-smelling sheets. Divested of his clothing, Jonathan followed.

Skin touching, they groaned.

"Make the ache go away," she pleaded softly.

Impatiently, frantically, she sought his lips. Opening her own, she sipped at his darting tongue. The purring noise escaped into his mouth.

"I have to slow down," he muttered in her ear.

"No!" she protested, raking her hands down his back and pulling him on top.

"Jaycee, honey. I've missed you . . . wanted you . . ." His hands kneaded her breasts as he gently mouthed one, then the other.

A delicious pain coursed through her, making her arch and thrust against him.

"Don't," she heard. But her writhing, arching hips didn't. The small hand that dipped below his waist ignored the command. Fingers guiding him into the aching void didn't hear the audible gasp.

"Oh, God, Jaycee."

Twisting her hips, clutching his, she held on tightly. Just as she was rediscovering the building peaks of their passion, she felt him remove her hands and spread them straight out beside her. He tensed, then withdrew.

"No," she called, struggling to free her hands.

"Too fast," he groaned in a self-depreciating voice. Holding both of her hands in one of his, he freed his other hand to stroke her from shoulder to waist.

"Please, Jonathan," she begged. "Even if you hate me, please don't stop now."

"Shh, darlin'," he whispered. His hand slipped below her waist to the center of her womanhood. "Shh, shh," he crooned, rubbing his lightly whiskered cheek across her stomach.

"Jonathan," she gasped as the fires began to eat at her insides. She was soaring. He was arousing her to a pitch she couldn't control or deny. "Jonathan!" she screamed, arching her hips to meet him. He released her hands and she held tightly to him. He thrust once, deeply, completely, shouting her name.

"Yes. Hold me, love. Don't let go." Jonathan's voice was shaking with emotion. Stretching over her length, he nuzzled the hard, rosy peaks of her breasts.

"You are delicious," he said, suckling her breasts tenderly, then he groaned and rose to take her lips. Slowly, with care, he pulled away slightly and caressed and kneaded her sensitized breasts until she thought they would burst.

"Again, love. Together all the way this time," he murmured. "Open your eyes. Let me see the copper fire."

Slowly she opened them. They glowed with contentment. "You are a wonderful lover," she said huskily.

A wide smile accompanied a deep chuckle. "You didn't think that a few minutes ago," he said, pulling away slightly.

Wrapping her legs around his hips, Jaycee asked, "Why?"

"Because, my dear, you are a wanton hussy."

"Hmmm." A quick thrust took any words right out of her mouth.

"Because it has been two very long, lonely months," he further explained.

"Mmmm," she responded for the same reason.

"Because you would have been a very *frustrated* wanton hussy if I hadn't."

"Men aren't supposed to be able to . . ."

Jonathan chuckled at the naive remark. "Hon, if

a man wants his woman satisfied, he can slow the pace. That is part of loving . . . caring . . ."

She wasn't interested in any more reasons. Writhing, arching, twisting, she began the climb again. Imprisoning his hips, she took Jonathan with her. She loved this man. Without him she could survive, but that wasn't living. It was merely existing. Poles apart from the heights he was carrying her to.

Satiated, released from physical desires, they lay together, murmuring love words back and forth.

"Jonathan? Why did you hesitate to take me into the house?"

"I was caught between wanting to make passionate love and, well, you distracted me from my reason for hiding in the shadows."

"I was hoping this *was* the reason," she replied, tweaking his flat male nipple.

Whipping the sheet back, he leaned out of the bed, picking up his hastily discarded slacks. Searching, he pulled a small green velvet box from the pocket. He switched the lamp on. Rolling over, he placed the jeweler's box on his chest. A wide smile stretched his lips.

"That," he said, pointing to the box, "is why I came."

Dark eyes sparkled. It was a ring box. Her first impulse was to grab it and open the lid as quickly as possible. Reaching for it, she saw the smug look on Jonathan's features and rested her palm on his waist.

"Aren't you supposed to ask a question first?" she asked, wanting to hear the words.

Rolling to his side, propping his head on one hand,

he watched the soft velvet covering of the ring box nestle against her breast. "I do have a question I want to ask."

Jaycee held her breath, closed her eyes, and waited.

"Would we be here if Scotty hadn't told you?"

Dark eyes popped open. "What?"

"You heard the question."

"Well! I don't know what Scotty was supposed to have told me," she answered tartly, disgusted with the unromantic question.

"Don't play dumb. He told you about the date on the release form, didn't he?" His tone was dead serious. "Otherwise you would never have come to the lecture."

"Jonathan, I don't know what you are jabbering about. You are in my bed because that is where I want you. Men!" she complained loudly. She was thoroughly exasperated. *Here I am waiting for a proposal and he wants to rake over cold ashes!*

Giving a whoop, tossing his head back, he roared with laughter. *"You don't know!* If you had read the release form *carefully . . ."*

"But I did," she protested. "Over and over as a matter of fact."

"The date. Did you notice the date?"

"The date was important?"

"You bet, lady. Before you brought the check in, *I* had already paid the taxes. I couldn't keep the shop from closing, but by paying the taxes I did get it opened immediately."

"You paid the taxes," she asked, astounded.

184

Jonathan nodded his head. "Then when you didn't return my calls, I figured . . ."

"I'd welshed on my end of the bribe!" she said, completing the sentence angrily.

". . . *you'd* had a holiday fling," he finished.

Echoing her own fears, she saw the vulnerability on his face.

"I love you with all my heart, my body, my soul, Jaycee." Picking up the velvet box, he opened it with one hand. A large diamond solitaire in a Tiffany setting twinkled brilliantly. "Will you marry me, Jaycee Warner?" he asked, giving her a deliciously sexy wink. "The ring is a bribe," he added.

She didn't need to answer. She'd done that earlier when she had invited him into her home. With a quick wink of her own, she plucked the ring from its satin bed. "Only if you promise to put a padlock"—his eyebrow rose—". . . on the door of this house . . . with us inside."

And he did. Later.

LOOK FOR NEXT MONTH'S
CANDLELIGHT ECSTASY ROMANCES®

COMING
IN
AUGUST—

Beginning this August, you can read a romance series unlike all the others — CANDLELIGHT ECSTASY SUPREMES! Ecstasy Supremes are the stories you've been waiting for—longer, and more exciting, filled with more passion, adventure and intrigue. Breathtaking and unforgettable. Love, the way you always imagined it could be. Look for CANDLELIGHT ECSTASY SUPREMES, four new titles every other month.

NEW DELL

TEMPESTUOUS EDEN,
by Heather Graham.
$2.50

Blair Morgan—daughter of a powerful man, widow of a famous senator—sacrifices a world of wealth to work among the needy in the Central American jungle and meets Craig Taylor, a man she can deny nothing.

EMERALD FIRE,
by Barbara Andrews
$2.50

She was stranded on a deserted island with a handsome millionaire—what more could Kelly want? Love.

NEW DELL

CANDLELIGHT
Ecstasy Supreme

LOVERS AND PRETENDERS,
by Prudence Martin
$2.50

Christine and Paul—looking for new lives on a cross-country jaunt, were bound by lies and a passion that grew more dangerously honest with each passing day. Would the truth destroy their love?

WARMED BY THE FIRE,
by Donna Kimel Vitek
$2.50

When malicious gossip forces Juliet to switch jobs from one television network to another, she swears an office romance will never threaten her career again—until she meets superstar anchorman Marc Tyner.

Desert Hostage

Diane Dunaway

Behind her is England and her first innocent encounter with love. Before her is a mysterious land of forbidding majesty. Kidnapped, swept across the deserts of Araby, Juliette Barclay sees her past vanish in the endless, shifting sands. Desperate and defiant, she seeks escape only to find harrowing danger, to discover her one hope in the arms of her captor, the Shiek of El Abadan. Fearless and proud, he alone can tame her. She alone can possess his soul. Between them lies the secret that will bind her to him forever, a woman possessed, a slave of love.

A DELL BOOK   11963-4 $3.95